TEARDROPS AND REST STOPS

A Warm Your Heart Romantic Comedy about
Two Travelers and the Dog Who Judges Them

LARK GRIFFING

WIND LARK
PUBLISHING

ISBN-13: **978-0-9988719-5-0**

Edited by Wing Family Editing

Cover Design by Wicked Whale Publishing

For my friends who taught us to teardrop camp:
Rich, Val, Chuck, Barb, Ken, Pat,
and the rest of the Tearjerker gang.

Chapter 1

Joe cruised over the causeway leaving Assateague Island and Ruby behind. He glanced in the rearview mirror. The little teardrop trailer he pulled traveled smoothly behind his truck. Everything was well. Except it wasn't. Ruby wasn't following him. Not that he expected it. He had only known that amazing woman for a few days, but he had hoped she would take him up on the adventure.

He wasn't going to give up.

He turned on the GPS and started the course he had set up the night before. The Florida Keys. He had a client, a friend, who wanted his hotel photographed for an upcoming marketing campaign. Joe had been looking forward to the job. He loved the Keys, and he was planning on doing some fishing and shooting some photographs to bulk up his stock photo portfolio. Now, he wasn't as excited about it. He was going to be alone.

He had been alone for the past eight months, ever since his fiancée broke up with him to run off with a body builder. He had been bitter, angry, and bewildered. Then he met Ruby. Now, all he felt was alone and that he was missing something, and that something was her. And her little dog. Her annoying, protective, jealous reincarnated husband of a little dog, George.

Joe laughed thinking about the first time he thought the damn dog was Ruby's husband come back to life in the body of a dog. It was an insane idea. Ludicrous, and he knew it. But the damn dog knew what he was thinking and even got in the way when Joe tried to make a move on Ruby. Damn dog. On the other hand, that damn dog had saved her life, and Joe would never forget it.

Eight hours later, he pulled into Santee State Park in South Carolina. He had reservations for the night. He backed his little teardrop camper into his site and crawled inside to his bed. It was still early, but he was tired. He had a sandwich he picked up earlier, so he flipped up the side table attached to his door and put the sandwich on it.

He wasn't hungry.

He stared at his cell phone, willing it to give him some indication that Ruby might be thinking about him. There was nothing.

What did he expect? He just met the woman.

But still.

His fingers hovered over the screen.

Text her.

He shook his head at himself.

Just text her. Let her know that you are thinking about her.

He sighed.

He unwrapped his sandwich and took a bite.

I wonder what she's having for dinner? I wonder if she's eating alone? Maybe a friendly neighbor asked to join her. After all, that's how this all got started.

He pulled up her last text. His fingers hesitated.

Just let her know she's on your mind. No pressure. Just a friendly thought.

He took another bite of his sandwich. It was a lonely bite. No Ruby. No George to try to win over with a morsel or two.

His fingers tapped on his phone.

Follow your heart.

Joe hit send.

Chapter 2

R uby stared down at the text on her phone. It was the umpteenth time in two days that she had looked at it. *Follow your heart.* It's what her husband told her when he died. It's what a friend had told her when she was so lost she didn't know where to turn. It was the phrase that had come to her in her sleep. *Follow your heart.*

But did she know her heart? She thought she did. She always wanted to be wild and free, exploring and having non-stop adventures.

She had put that dream aside when she had married George. Dear, sweet George. Solid and steadfast. An accountant. A planner. A man who loved his recliner and his losing Cleveland sports teams. George. The man who knew her heart even when she thought he didn't. The man who knew he was going to die, so he secretly bought Ruby her teardrop camper so she could follow her impetuous dream. The man with the foresight to open an insurance policy that would provide her with enough funds to keep her comfortable. Dear, sweet George. Dear, dead George.

Now that she was free, she fiercely wished she wasn't. She would trade it all to have her George back.

A tear meandered down her cheek, ending in the corner of her mouth. Salty.

George gently licked it away.

George, the dog. Not George, the husband.

She reached over and scratch the little Border Terrier mix behind the ears. He stretched his neck out and smiled, his eyes half closed.

George had come to her at a national forest campsite. He was a dirty stray, and she was alone. She cleaned him up, discovering a leather collar with the name *George* embossed in the leather.

That threw Ruby. She didn't want to have anything to do with the dog, but a kind forest ranger and the persistent pup had convinced Ruby to take a chance on the mutt. Now, they were inseparable.

George had very strong opinions on men. Most of them he didn't like. He had raised his lip and snarled at Joe on many occasions.

Joe just laughed at him.

George let Joe know he wasn't amused.

Joe became uneasy when he realized the dog could read his mind. But he really couldn't. Could he?

Joe joked that George, the husband had come back reincarnated as George, the dog. Joe laughed about that, uneasily. It was just too strange.

Ruby was heading down to the Florida Keys, pulling her little teardrop camper. She was traveling toward Joe, but he didn't know it. She wasn't in a hurry. She was taking her time. Thinking.

They had just met. She wasn't ready for a relationship. She still missed her husband. She liked being free and alone, but she didn't always like being alone. She was conflicted.

She had George.

She was still lonely.

She drove toward Florida.

Somewhere in Georgia her phone rang. It was her boss, Laney. She wanted to let Ruby know that the article about Assateague Island was great, and they had selected some of Joe's photos to accompany it. She also had several more articles that needed Ruby's editing skills, and Ruby would find them in her inbox. Mostly, Laney was nosey and wanted to know if Ruby was alright, and what was up with this Joe guy. Was he just a professional contact, or was there something there?

Ruby deflected most of the questions, but Laney was good, and when they hung up, Laney was reminding her that Ruby had a lot of life ahead of her, and it was okay to consider relationships. Ruby ignored the hint.

The Jeep rolled south, pulling the trailer steadily, getting ever closer to the Florida Keys. Ruby had no idea where Joe was staying. She wasn't ready to find out. She wanted to discover the Keys on her own terms. If Joe was still around when she was ready to share the discovery, then so be it. If not, it was never meant to be.

Chapter 3

George whined softly beside Ruby. It was getting late, and he needed to find a tree. She looked down at him as he sat on the passenger seat looking out the front window. He turned to her a woofed.

"Okay, buddy. I'll look for a place to stop. Can you hang on?"

George wagged his tail and lay back down on the seat. Ruby knew what he needed. He would be patient, and she would take care of him. Just as he would take care of her.

Like Joe would take care of her.

George growled softly.

"I'm looking. Hang on."

George closed his eyes and slept.

Ruby saw a sign. *Rest area two miles.* She would pull off and let George have a walk. She thought she might pull into the truck parking area and crawl into the camper to sleep for a bit.

Ruby snapped the leash on George and walked him into the dog area, being careful where she stepped. George looked at her with disgust in his eyes. He hated doggy bathrooms. He did his business, his lips curled in disgust the whole time.

"Good boy. I'll get you a treat, and then you need to wait while I use the restroom." George wagged his tail

Ruby gave him a puppy biscuit and closed and locked him in the teardrop. She made her way into the rest stop building.

After completing her business, she washed her hands and her face. She should stop for the night. She was kind of tired. She had never slept at a rest stop, but there was always a first time for everything.

On the way out, Ruby stopped at the counter and looked at the map under the plastic protector. She still had a long way to go. Florida was a very long state.

Next to the map was a large book, a register for people to write who they were and where they were from. Ruby glanced at it, amused at the people who would bother to write anything down. She wondered who would actually care.

Her eyes idly passed down the page.

Then stopped.

Joe Lerner . Keep driving south, Ruby.

Ruby started at the words. Blinked. Yep, they were still there. *Keep driving south.* What are the chances? *Ruby.*

She smiled at the warm feeling spreading through her belly. She thought of the night on the dune. The wild abandon she felt when Joe kissed her. The urging of her soul to continue, explore the freedom. Then she giggled, remembering the couple tripping over them in the dark.

Then, the inevitable guilt. George. Her devoted husband. The man who was happy just to have Ruby in his life.

When was it right to…not move on…that sounded wrong. To continue to live. She knew George wanted her to. Demanded that she do so, with his dying breath. But…it felt… like… Betrayal.

She traced the words with her finger, *keep driving south*, and bit her lip. She was tired. She could rest, or she could keep driving. South.

Two hours later, Ruby was struggling to keep her eyes open. According to her app, there was another rest stop in fifteen miles. If she could just stay awake that long.

It was stupid to have left the last rest stop and keep driving. She knew she was tired, but she had to admit to herself the truth. Something was calling her, driving her on... south. Joe.

"Don't cry for me Argentina. The truth is I never left you." Ruby sang at the top of her lungs trying desperately to stay awake. She had chugged a Pepsi an hour ago, but its effects were short lived. Now, singing was going to get her through.

George sighed heavily on the seat next to her.

"Come on buddy. You have to help keep me awake. Sing with me. *Through all my wild days, my mad existence...*"

George sat up and put a paw on Ruby's arm, as if to plead with her to stop her caterwauling.

"What? Oh, that's right. You never liked *Evita*. What would you rather have me sing? *Joseph and the Amazing Technicolor Dreamcoat*? That was always one of your favorites. Or *Les Mis*? No, too sad. Okay, *Joseph* it is.

"Some folks dream of the wonders they'll do. Before their time on this planet is through. Some just don't have anything planned..."

George raised his head and howled along with Ruby as they drove south down the freeway.

Ruby forgot for a moment that it was George, the dog beside her.

Chapter 4

G eorge woke Ruby up by placing a paw on each of her shoulders and licking her lips. He knew that usually brought her out of a deep sleep. He had to go outside, and he was hungry. It was time to get this show on the road.

Ruby opened one eye to the Border Terrier's snout a half an inch from her face.

"Good lord, dog. What the heck did you eat last night? Your breath stinks."

Ruby drew the sheet over her head, playfully knocking the dog off of her and onto his pillow.

George grinned with satisfaction. Ruby missed the fact that he had found the remains of a particularly tasty burrito next to a garbage can last night. He chowed down on it quickly, licking the paper clean. Last night it had seemed like a great idea. This morning...not so much. He. Had. To. Go. Outside. NOW.

He nosed into the sheet and barked.

"I can see the green gas coming out of your mouth. You stink." Then Ruby gagged. The smell was horrendous. "Buddy, I don't think that was from your mouth. Hang on."

Ruby jumped out of bed and pulled on the pair of sweats she always kept ready. She slipped her feet into her flip flops and grabbed George's leash.

"Let's go, buddy. Oh my God. You really stink."

George wagged his tail and strained at the leash as they left the camper. He practically drug Ruby toward the garbage can. He was feeling pretty frantic and needed to find the perfect place to squat. Wait. This was good. Oh look. The burrito paper. Mid squat, George flipped his tongue out to give that magical waxed paper another swipe.

"LEAVE IT," Ruby yelled. "You ate that damn thing last night, didn't you?" she accused the dog who was currently being sick all over the lawn.

He looked over his shoulder at her sheepishly.

"It serves you right."

The dog squatted and walked, squatted and walked. A man made a clucking sound and looked at Ruby with disgust as he walked passed them. She shrugged and looked down. It suddenly dawned on her she didn't have a bag to pick up the giant piles of liquified excrement.

George made a final effort then dug his back legs into the dirt, shook himself, then trotted over to Ruby like nothing had happened at all.

"Great. Now I have to pick this stuff up." George just grinned at her and picked up the burrito wrapper in his mouth, trotting ahead of her with his prize. Ruby burst out laughing. "You're an ass."

Ruby dug around in the camper and produced a recycled grocery bag and her little backpacking shovel meant for dealing with her own issues in the woods.

"This is how much I love you, dog," Ruby grumbled on her way back to the offensive mess.

After she had taken care of the business and cleaned the shovel with some travel wipes she always carried, she locked

George in the camper and went into the rest stop facilities to take care of her own needs. When she got back, George was sitting at the door looking desperate.

"What? Again? Seriously?" She snapped the leash on George and led him outside, crossing the lawn and entering a woods in the back. "Have at it, buddy."

George obliged.

Again.

And Again.

"Um, George, we have a long way to go today. Is this going to be an all day thing?"

The dog looked at her apologetically. Demonstrated, and looked at her again with his ears down.

"I'm sorry. You probably feel miserable. Let's give it a try and see how you do. If it doesn't work, I'll find a place and we'll lay low for the day. And from now on, no more burritos for you."

Ruby boiled a small amount of rice for George to help with his stomach upset and put it in a bag in the Jeep Wrangler for later. She filled the dog's water bottle and her own and grabbed a couple of granola bars from the camper. Satisfied everything was ready, she checked her hitch and locked up the camper.

"Come on, George. Give it one more go before we leave." She walked the dog over to the woods again. George wandered around in circles for a while, then squatted and was sick again. "Buddy, I have a bad feeling about today."

She lifted the little dog and put him in the front passenger seat. Then she thought twice about it and lifted him down again. George looked up at her and whined.

Ruby rummaged in the back of the Jeep and came up with an old towel. She lay it across the seat and put George back where he belonged. He sniffed the towel and then lay down, snuggling his nose in the folds of the towel. He sighed and closed his eyes.

His tummy rumbled.

His eyes flew open.

He looked at Ruby then flew out of the Jeep and relieved himself again. Ruby sat on the Jeep's bumper and waited for her dog to finish. She was getting worried.

George walked stiff-legged back to the Jeep and jumped up on the seat. He lay back down again and closed his eyes. Ruby reached in to pet his head and scratched his ears.

"Feel better, buddy. Just let me know when you need to stop."

She got behind the wheel and pulled out of the rest stop heading south on the freeway.

Chapter 5

"Ruby, you're breaking up. What did you say George ate?"
"I think he found an old burrito behind a garbage
can at a rest stop. All I know is he has horrible diarrhea. When
I let him out this morning, he made a beeline for the garbage
can and started licking the burrito wrapper. Then all hell broke
loose. Is he going to be okay?"

Ruby smiled at the state trooper as she passed him, the
phone held down by her lap.

"Ruby? Ruby, did I lose you?" asked Rich, the veterinarian
who checked out George when he came to Ruby as a stray.

"Sorry, just passed a statie running radar. I can't remember
if this is a no cell phone state or not."

"Where are you?"

"We just crossed the line into Florida."

"Lucky. Where are you heading?"

"I'm going to the Florida Keys for a bit. If I ever get there.
We have been taking quite a few rests stops. Seriously, is
George going to be okay?"

They chatted for a few minutes, Ruby being delicately
descriptive about George's stool. Rich reminding Ruby to

make sure George drank enough water. Florida was hot, and diarrhea was dehydrating.

"I think he's probably going to be fine. All signs point to digestive upset at the hands of Mexican food. I think we've all been there. The boiled rice is perfect for him. If you can get hold of some boiled chicken, that should help, too. If he is still sick tomorrow, give me another call, and I'll help you find a vet to take him to wherever you are. Sound good?"

"Yes. Thank you so much, Rich. You're a good friend."

"Speaking of friends, have you talked to Adam lately?"

"Not for a month or so. How is he doing?"

"He's okay. He is still not ready for a long-term relationship, but honey, I think you would be great for him. Consider coming back for a visit. Besides, he needs to get his sister off his back again. She really wants to be an aunt." With Rich's laughter ringing in her ear, they said goodbye.

Ruby drove on, scratching George's head as he slept, remembering the weekend when George came into her life and the people who helped make that happen. Adam was the park ranger that drove her and the stray dog to the vet to have the little guy checked out. Rich was that vet. They were the ones who convinced Ruby to give George his forever home. Adam also used her shamelessly to pose as his girlfriend, so his sister would stop bugging him about being single.

Had she met Adam at a later time, when they were both more ready for a relationship, they would have been a good fit. Adam was easy going, easy on the eyes, and was easy to laugh. They were comfortable with each other from the start.

Comfortable.

Like she was with George. She loved him, with all her heart. He loved her with all his heart, soul, and life. Ruby was his everything. Ruby was George's air.

George was Ruby's husband.

That made her sad. She brushed away the tear that was

threatening to squeeze from her eye and run down her cheek. George opened his eyes and licked her hand.

They drove on. South.

Ruby pulled into Anastasia State Park. She had called while on the road and was lucky to score a campsite for the evening. As she signed in, she looked at the brochures in the wire rack that touted everything she could do and see in the area. Maybe she should take a day and rest and let George recover. The silver-haired lady sporting a pink sweatshirt with a flamingo drinking a daiquiri checked her computer and slotted Ruby in for a second night. It was meant to be.

Ruby and George were going to rest and play tourist.

Chapter 6

R uby opened her eyes feeling the hot breath of George on her lips. He was standing on her chest, and when he saw her eyes were open, he licked her face then jumped down and ran to the door. *Uh oh. Not again*, thought Ruby.

She hurried, pulling on her sweats and flip flops and snapped the leash on George. This was becoming the routine of the morning as George waited anxiously for Ruby to get him out the door.

She stepped outside with George right behind her. He pulled on his leash and led her to a bush behind the teardrop. Then he lifted his leg with a look of relief on his face.

"That's what you had to do? That was the emergency?" Ruby watched her dog's face as he grinned at her. He finished and trotted around sniffing the area. He lifted his leg again.

"Remind me to check your water dish. You must have drunk a lot last night. Poor guy, you were probably really dehydrated, huh?"

George trotted up to her and sat up. He clearly felt he deserved a treat.

"Are you sure your tummy is ready for jerky strips? How about some rice and chicken? Will that work?"

George barked a happy reply and led her to the camper. Ruby warmed the remaining rice and chicken in the microwave just enough to take the chill off. When it was done, she checked the temperature then put it on the floor for George. She cleaned the water bowl, which was bone dry, and put fresh water in it. George looked at her out of the corner of his eye as he wolfed down the rice and wagged his tail in appreciation.

"You look a lot better today, buddy. Let's hope that processes in your gut the way it's supposed to. I'm going to take a shower. Can you be a good boy while I do that?"

George wagged his tail in acknowledgment.

Ruby gathered her shower tote and towel and locked the camper behind her. The little teardrop had a tiny bathroom that included a shower. Ruby would have to stand in front of the toilet or sit on it and the shower sprayed the whole bathroom. It was extremely clever, but cramped. It was a way to keep the bathroom clean, but when good facilities were available, Ruby would use the campground showers.

Ruby walked to the showers, her flip flops slapping against her feet. Children were riding bikes and a young couple was walking their dog. Ruby smiled to herself, feeling lucky that she could take her job on the road and enjoy traveling at her own pace. She was beginning to settle in to this life, and she was happy. Another couple passed her holding hands and talking about what sites they were going to take in that day. *I do miss that*, she thought to herself. *That's why you are driving south, darlin'.* She smiled as she pulled open the door to the shower house.

"George, are you okay?" Ruby called as she unlocked the camper door. Her hair was twisted up in a towel and her skin glowed from being freshly scrubbed.

George jumped down from his pillow and nosed the door.

"You need to go out again? How did your breakfast sit?"

George wagged his tail and waited for her to snap his leash back on. Once again, he trotted back to the bushes where he promptly lifted his leg. He then turned his back to her and completed the rest of his business. Ruby was relieved to see that George was back to normal.

"Yay, George," she praised. He looked at her, embarrassed, then stalked past her with as much dignity as he could muster.

"Sorry pal. That was uncalled for, but I am glad you are feeling better."

Ruby brewed some coffee and made an egg and English muffin for herself. She carried breakfast out to the picnic table, along with the brochures she picked up the night before. George followed her.

"What do you say we check out St. Augustine today? We can go see the Fountain of Youth and Castillo de San Marcos National Monument. It looks like you can come with me, but we just can't go inside the fort. I'm okay with that. Sound good?"

George listened to her with his ears cocked, tilting his head this way and that as she talked. When she was down to her last bite of muffin, he sat up and begged, pawing the air and looking pitiful.

"I don't know buddy. It's not a good idea with your stomach and all." She looked at the disappointed dog and hesitated. It was such a small bite.

Ruby's cell phone rang.

She sat the muffin down and picked up the phone.

"Hello, Rich," she said, smiling as she saw the vet's number.

"How is George doing this morning?"

"Everything seems to be… um… coming out normally," she said. She looked down at the crumb of muffin. *Busted*, she thought.

23

"Good. Keep him away from people food for a while. Give him more rice and chicken with just a little of his dry food mixed in. By tomorrow he should be just fine with his normal dry. Just remember to give him lots of water, especially in that Florida heat."

"Okay, I will. Thanks for checking up on him."

"Anytime, Ruby. By the way, I saw Adam last night. We went out for wings and his sister was there. I made a point to tell him you said hello and you were thinking about him. He says thank you, and he owes you for that."

Ruby chuckled as she hung up the phone. Adam was a very nice man. One day, he would be a great catch for the right girl.

Chapter 7

George trotted along smartly on his leash next to Ruby. They made the perfect tourist pair as they explored the grounds of the Fountain of Youth. Ruby was wearing a pair of white capris with aqua flip flops. She threw caution to the wind with her aqua and white striped shirt sprinkled with a smattering of pink flamingos. Her auburn hair was pulled into a French braid that trailed down her back, and she sported a pair of white framed sunglasses. She laughed at her reflection as she passed a plate glass window. Her dead husband, George, would have been pained by her outfit. It was a little too dashing for him.

She felt wonderful in it. She smiled wistfully. Even if he wouldn't have liked it, he would have still told her she was beautiful.

Yes, I would have.

His voice came to her a clear as a bell.

She looked down at her little dog. George looked up at her innocently. He wagged his tail then delicately sniffed the droppings of another dog.

"George, leave it." Ruby scolded. George trotted happily on.

They both drank water from the Fountain of Youth and, on a whim, Ruby asked a young woman to take a picture of her and George under the entrance archway to the attraction.

An idea was forming in Ruby's head.

After they left there, they went to see the Castillo de San Marcos. Ruby marveled at the size of the fortress built so long ago out of coquina. Once again, Ruby asked a stranger to kindly take a picture of her and George, this time with the historic structure in the background.

When they tired of the sightseeing, George and Ruby headed into town where they walked the streets and window shopped. A remarkable number of stores welcomed George, and in return for their kindness, he made certain he was well behaved.

A small restaurant with a sidewalk patio had a large bowl of fresh water out for dogs to stop and have a drink. Ruby decided that it was the perfect place to have dinner, so she and George settled into a patio table and enjoyed the next couple of hours eating conch chowder, fresh grouper, and peanut butter pie. Ruby let George have a tiny taste of grouper and a finger full of the pie. Her waitress, Sally, an older, bosomy lady who fell in love with George, fed him puppy biscuits and crusts of bread. Ruby hoped George wouldn't pay for the indulgence.

Sally took a picture of George in Ruby's lap with the plate of Grouper complete with a puppy biscuit garnish.

"Are you done for the day, buddy?" Ruby asked, as she lingered over the last bite of pie.

George thumped his tail against her thigh. He was snuggled in her lap, hidden by the table cloth. He was dog tired but happy.

Ruby picked up her phone as she popped the last of the pie in her mouth. Should she, or shouldn't she? She thought for a minute, then selected three of the best pictures of her and George at the fort, dinner, and Fountain of Youth. Before she could change her mind, she quickly texted them to Joe without a word of explanation.

He would figure out where they were.

He had the next move.

Chapter 8

Joe was contemplating the fish on the end of his line, or rather the glimpse of fish he got as it flashed toward the surface and dived deep, straining against the line.

The fight was getting old. He just wasn't into it. Ben was looking mournfully into his empty beer can.

"Are you going to bring that damn fish in or not?" Ben reached into the cooler to grab another beer and came up empty.

"I suppose. He will be mighty tasty on my plate."

"Well, we're out of beer, so finish this."

Joe turned his attention to the fish again when his phone indicated he'd gotten a couple of texts.

I can't believe I have service out here, Joe thought. He glanced down at his pocket.

"Pay attention. You're going to lose dinner."

At that moment, Joe felt the tension in the line change. He reeled quickly, drawing the fish closer.

Ben jumped forward and neatly netted the fish.

"Hot damn, Joe. That is one hell of a grouper."

They admired the fish for another minute then tossed it in the cooler with his unfortunate friends.

"My friend, we are out of beer and out of patience. Let's go eat." Joe set about putting away his fishing gear as Ben started the boat engines. Ben banked the boat and headed back to the marina in Islamorada.

As Joe settled into his seat, he remembered the texts. He reached into his pocket, pulling out the phone.

"My friend, you're on vacation. Put that thing away."

Joe just grinned and pressed the code to unlock the phone. Ruby's name showed up on his screen.

Ruby.

Ruby sent him a text.

All of the sudden, Joe sat up straighter. The next minute, he was staring at Ruby's beautiful smile and George's arrogant chin lift as they posed in front of the fortress in St. Augustine.

"Hey, Joe. Is everything okay?"

Joe didn't answer as he flipped through the pictures she sent. Ruby and George in front of the Fountain of Youth, Ruby and George eating at an outdoor patio.

Ruby and George. They were in Florida. They were heading south, and she was teasing him.

He liked that.

"JOE. Is everything okay?" Ben shouted, concerned for his friend, until he saw the smile teasing at the corners of Joe's mouth.

Ah... Ben thought...*it must be a girl.*

"So, what's her name?" asked Ben from the back of the boat.

"Hmmm?" asked Joe, not lifting his head.

"You've been moping for days. You did brilliant work, taking pictures of my hotel, but you didn't get a damn bit of joy out of it. You usually get a kick out of producing great shots. I took you for fifty bucks playing pool last night, and you didn't care. And today, I take you out for some of the best sport fishing in the United States, and you consider not even fighting the damn fish the good Lord had the kindness to grace your line. Now, you get a measly little text and you're actually smiling. Maybe even grinning. So what gives?"

"It's nothing. Just a lady I met up at Assateague Island. She has a teardrop camper, too. No big deal."

"No big deal, my ass." Ben leaned forward straining to see Joe's phone. "Wait, that's not just a text. That's a picture. Show me."

Joe cleared the screen and looked up innocently at Ben. "What?"

"Oh no. You'll show me the picture. Especially if you want to get back to shore."

"You're full of empty threats, my friend."

"Bet me. Show me the picture or I'll throw your ass overboard...and keep your fish."

Joe laughed again until he caught the look in Ben's eyes. *He couldn't possibly be serious.*

"I'm serious, buddy. I'll toss you in the drink with your cell phone. There isn't enough rice in the world to dry out your phone after taking a bath in the ocean, now let's just get this over with and show me the lady."

Joe opened the text again and wordlessly handed the phone to Ben.

Ben gave a low whistle of admiration.

"You do know how to pick 'em. Look at that hair, and those..."

"Stop," Joe warned, murder in his eyes.

"Holy crap. This isn't just some lady. You love this lady. Are you telling me you're over Julia the junkyard dog, and you've fallen for the lady with the red hair?"

"Is that what you call her?" Joe smirked at the reference

For the first time, the mention of Julia didn't cause a pain in Joe's heart. For the first time he didn't care that she had run off with the body builder. Hallelujah, he was over his fiancée. God bless, Ruby.

The sun was low in the sky when the boat came into dock. Joe quickly cleaned the fish as Ben took care of the boat. Together they carried the equipment up to the house where Laura was waiting for them.

Ben kissed his very pregnant wife and pulled a pan out of the cupboard to start sautéing the fish. Laura basted rosemary potatoes with butter then put them back in the oven to stay warm along with a loaf of fresh Italian bread.

"Hey Laura," said Joe as he came around and kissed her cheek. She rose on her tiptoes so Joe didn't have to bend down so far. Laura was a petite Italian lady with a gift for creating food and a wicked sense of humor.

"Hello, Joe. Ben said that you did a great job on the hotel pictures. I'd love to see them."

"I'll set up my laptop and show them to you after dinner, but those potatoes and that bread smell amazing."

Laura swatted at Joe with her towel and told him and Ben to go wash up, she would watch the fish.

Ben beat Joe back and he was whispering to Laura about the mystery lady in the text when Joe appeared.

"Ben spilling the beans about my personal life?" asked Joe as he took the plates from Laura's hands and started setting the table.

"He just said some lady texted you a couple of pictures. He said she has nice auburn hair and a really nice set of…"

"Wow, both of you?" Joe interrupted.

"He also said she has kind of a ratty looking dog."

"That is no way to talk about George," said Joe.

"George? What kind of name is George for a dog?" Laura said wrinkling her nose.

"If you only knew," murmured Joe under his breath.

Chapter 9

Over dinner, Joe gave Laura and Ben the lowdown on Ruby, her teardrop trailer, and her dog.

"You mean you just drove away and left her at Assateague Island so you could get here to photograph our hotel?" said Laura incredulously. "You could have taken a few more days. We could have waited."

"Yeah, Joe. If this lady can get you to stop thinking about that witch of an ex-fiancée, I approve of her."

"I needed to give her time. Her husband died, and she is just now thinking about coming out of that space and finding her new life. I'm not even sure if she knows it yet."

Laura started to smile.

"So, you're making sure she misses you. Not a bad plan, but she's a woman. She'll see through you." Laura watched Joe's face, searching for the sadness that had been there the last time they saw him. It wasn't there. He was over that horrible woman. She was actually happy the witch ran away with the body builder. Laura never liked Julia and figured it was going to end badly. She was grateful it ended before the wedding. It was less messy for her dear friend this way. Still, it had left him shell-shocked, deeply hurt. She needed to meet this Ruby girl and get a feel for this one. Laura was not going to let some woman hurt her friend again. No way. No how.

Joe showed Laura the hotel pictures, and she completely approved. She selected several to put into the brochure.

"I like these for the brochure, and I'm thinking this one for a post card? What do you think?" She was pointing at a beautiful shot with the hotel bathed in late evening light, a pink sunset behind. In the foreground a pelican rested on a post near the marina. The scene was tranquil and inviting.

"That's one of my favorites," said Joe. "It makes me want to plop my ass in the sand and sip on a mojito."

"A mojito? What the hell? Since when do you drink mojito's?" scoffed Ben, as he took a swig from his beer

"Ruby makes the best damn mojitos I've ever tasted."

"Ah, Ruby again," smiled Laura.

Joe looked uncomfortable, suddenly aware that he was wearing his heart on his sleeve. *Oh shit. I've got it bad.*

"So, you said she's in Florida. Can I assume she's following you and considering meeting up with you?" Laura was scheming.

"It would appear that way."

"Well, there's room for another camper parked next to yours out near the mangroves. There's another electric hookup isn't there Ben?"

"Yeah, we can make it work."

"Whoa guys. I know what you're doing. You're not matchmaking, and I'm not going to be under your scrutiny if Ruby comes. Seriously?"

"So, Joe. I made some homemade key lime pie. Would you like some?" said Laura, sweetly.

"Damn it, yes. And if you think you can keep me around

by plying me with your cooking...well, shit, maybe you can. We'll see. Ruby might not even come. She may change her mind. She still has a lot of Florida to drive through.

Chapter 10

Ruby hitched up the little trailer and made sure everything was secure before she told George to hop in the Jeep. He was feeling one hundred percent, and they were both eager to be on their way.

In the middle of the night a text had come in from Joe. *Nice pictures. You guys look great. Keep driving south, Ruby.*

She was going to take him up on that. It was only a little over five hours to Key Largo, the beginning of the island chain or keys that led to Key West, but Ruby wasn't in a hurry. She refused to let the tugging in her heart hurry her along her journey. She had never seen the everglades, so that was her next stop.

"George, we are going to explore the everglades. Do me a favor and don't get eaten by an alligator. Deal?"

George looked at her, cocking his head. He wagged his tail at her enthusiasm. Ruby seemed happier lately. She smiled. George liked that.

"I think we need to buy another kayak, buddy. I still can't believe mine got totaled at Assateague."

Ruby had been kayaking the coastline with George when a jet skier plowed into her kayak, dumping her and George into the ocean. The jet skier kept going, never stopping to see the damage he had done. George used every bit of strength he had to tow an unconscious Ruby to shore, then ran and found Joe, bringing him back to help Ruby.

"Maybe we can find one before we go into the National Park. Tell you what. Let's stop for lunch and gas, and we'll check the internet to see what we can find out."

Ruby pulled off the freeway and found a gas station. As she filled up the Jeep, she saw a small coffee shop next door. The owner welcomed George, so Ruby fortified herself with a tall coffee with a mocha shot and a grilled cheese sandwich. They sat at a small table while Ruby explored her options at the park.

"There's a place near Homestead where we can look for a new kayak, and it looks like we might be able to get a campsite for tonight, George. We'll have to hit the road so we can make time, but let me call and find out if we can reserve a spot."

Ruby's head was bent over her phone looking for the number to call when she heard George growling and felt him lean against her leg. She looked up to see a man approaching her table.

"Enough, George. Be nice." George chewed his growl for a second, then quieted. He stood with his back to Ruby, squarely facing off the stranger.

"I'm sorry. George is just very protective."

"I see that. No problem. My name is Greg. I just stopped by to refill the puppy biscuit jar here. It looks like George here was robbed of a treat." Greg smiled and held out a peace offering for George. "May I give it to him? It's homemade and all natural. A very healthy dog treat."

"Of course. Thank you. George sit."

George sat and considered the stranger, his left lip lifted in distain. Greg waited patiently, stretching out his hand with the treat toward the dog.

George's nose twitched. A strand of drool escaped from the black flappy stuff on the side of George's mouth. He had the decency to look embarrassed.

"Come on, little guy. You know you want it."

George lifted his right paw then stopped himself and set it down, his dignity restored. *No, you are going to come to me,* thought the little dog. He growled lightly, making a point.

Startled, the man looked at the dog. They stared at each other. The tip of George's tail wagged the tiniest bit. He knew he was winning.

"He's a stubborn one...and smart." Greg moved closer and held the biscuit in front of George's muzzle.

George assumed an innocent look and took the treat politely turning his back on Greg. He curled up on the floor behind Ruby and crunched on the biscuit.

"I couldn't help but hearing you talking to your dog. I heard you say you were needing to buy a kayak. What are you looking for?"

"Well, I had an ocean kayak before and I liked it, but it's a bit long and heavy for me to put on my Jeep myself."

"My son has a recreational kayak for sale. He bought himself a new fiberglass touring kayak and was hoping to recoup some cash by selling his old kayak. It's just next door if you want to see it."

"Next door?"

"Yes, I own the bakery. I make the puppy biscuits and the pastries Danny sells here in the coffee shop. So, you want to check out the kayak?"

"What do you think George? Should we go check it out?"

George came out from behind Ruby's legs licking his chops.

He walked over to Greg and regarded him, looking into his eyes. Greg returned the look, steady and kind. George wagged his tail and turned to Ruby.

Woof.

"Okay. Let's go check it out."

Chapter 11

G reg helped Ruby secure the kayak to the top of the Jeep, shaking her hand when they were done.

"Have fun with her, and be safe," said Greg.

"I will, and thank you. I think this is going to be perfect."

Greg slipped a bag of pastries and puppy biscuits into her Jeep, scratching George on the top of the head.

"You need to lighten up, fella. You're going to miss out on a lot of puppy biscuits if you don't start making friends easier."

George curled his lip at Greg and growled lightly. Greg just laughed. George sneezed then wagged his tail. He was just messing with Greg. The dog enjoyed it.

Fortified and with camping reservations all set up, Ruby and George turned south driving ever closer to the Florida Keys and the possibility of seeing Joe.

After hitting traffic around Miami, Ruby turned toward Homestead and the Everglades National Park. She pulled into the parking lot at Anhinga trail. She had about two and a half hours until sunset, and she still had to drive to the campgrounds at Flamingo, an hour away. Still, she knew George needed to go out and she needed to stretch her legs. This was one of the few trails in the park George was permitted to go on, so she wanted to take some time and explore the park.

Ruby tucked a poop bag in her pocket and snapped George's leash on. At the last minute, she grabbed the bug spray out of the teardrop and sprayed herself liberally.

They started down the paved path, Ruby keeping a watch out for alligators.

"George, you need to be a good dog. There really are alligators here, so you need to stay close. He looked up at her grinning and wagging his tail. He strutted down the path as if to say, *I'm tough. I'm not afraid of anything.*

Ruby snapped some pictures of a group of cormorants drying their wings while perched on some branches that stretched over the water. Under the water lurked an alligator. The sight of the gator gave Ruby chills, and she pulled George a little closer to her. As they continued down the path, they saw three turtles sunning themselves on the edge of the path. As they looped back in the direction of the car, George stopped and growled.

"What's wrong, buddy?" Ruby looked around and saw nothing. George started barking, looking over the side of the path toward the water. He was trying to sound tough, but he crowded against Ruby's legs and he was shaking.

"Hey George, what is it?" Ruby crouched down to pet her frightened dog. Her eyes drifted over to where George was looking, and she realized that a gator was staring back at her as he lay low on his belly on the side of the path.

Ruby felt an electric thrill of fear jolt through her body. George sensed the change in her and whimpered. The gator seemed to raise up a bit, as if he were doing a slow push up.

Ruby scooped George up in her arms and walked quickly past the gator, skirting around him as far away as she could. All of the sudden, the allure of the everglades was fading. She had planned on kayaking into the sea of grass, the romantic idea appealing to her. Now, coming face to face with an alligator made her rethink the idea.

They made it back to the Jeep without any incidents. Once she got in, she laughed shakily. George jumped into her lap and licked her chin.

"George, millions of people have hiked this path, and the gators have not hurt anyone. Yet, both you and I freaked out there. We're wusses."

George shook himself and jumped into his seat. He looked out the window as if nothing happened. When Ruby didn't start the Jeep, he turned and looked at her. She was staring straight ahead. George barked breaking her reverie.

"Sorry, buddy. That just really scared me. All my life I wanted adventure, but when I'm faced with it, I don't have as much courage as I imagine I will. What does that say about me and my dreams? I just don't know…" Ruby's voice trailed off as she started the car and drove on toward Flamingo.

Ruby pulled into her campsite as the sun set in the west. Her campsite overlooked the Florida bay which was tinted pink from the setting sun.

She quickly set up her camper and pulled out camp chairs for George and herself. They sat outside the camper in the quiet and watched the pink on the water fade to an inky darkness.

She scanned the pictures on her phone and selected one of an alligator and one of the pink waters of the bay. She sent them on to Joe.

Chapter 12

R uby woke up to a scratchy throat. Normally an early riser, Ruby rolled over and fell back to sleep.

An hour later, George pawed Ruby. She roused herself and let him outside. She tethered him to a line she had attached to the teardrop. After seeing the gator the night before, she decided she didn't want her dog to go off exploring and end up as a snack for the primitive looking reptile.

She heated water for some tea, let the dog back in, and took a shower as she let the tea steep. The hot shower cleared her head, and she was feeling a little better as she toasted an English muffin and poured some kibbles in George's bowl.

She had planned to go kayaking, but the alligator and the way she was feeling made her rethink her plan.

"Hey buddy," she croaked, her voice deeper than usual. "I'm going to head over to the visitor center to see what we can do today in the park. You're not welcome there, so eat your breakfast while I'm gone, and we will do something when I get back."

Ruby grabbed a couple of maps and brochures at the visitor center and decided that the everglades just wasn't the place for a dog. A man overheard her talking to a ranger, and he told her about an airboat ride company that would actually let her take George. She looked up the name of the company on her phone and secured a reservation for the two of them. After they were done with that, she figured she would drive around with George and just take in the scenery then head out toward Key Largo.

The airboat ride wasn't until later in the afternoon, so they hung around the campground and explored the shore of the bay until it was time to leave.

Ruby and George enjoyed an afternoon of a private airboat ride with a colorful local named Rabbit. Rabbit and George took to each other. George didn't see Rabbit as a threat. Most of the ride, George sat in Rabbit's lab, his ears flapping in the wind. He started to bark at the large white egrets, but Rabbit shushed him, and he remained quiet for the rest of the ride. Ruby couldn't get over how polite and accommodating the dog was.

Ruby enjoyed the ride, but her throat was getting really sore, and her face was feeling painful and swollen. By the time they arrived back at her camper, she was feeling out of sorts and her teeth hurt.

"Damn, George. I think I am getting a cold. Who gets a cold in the summer in Florida?" Digging in the center console, Ruby found a small pack of tissue. She attempted to blow her nose, but only came up unsatisfied with a lot of pressure in her sinuses and face.

George looked at her with concern.

"No worries, buddy. It's just a cold. Before we leave, we need to send the pictures of us with Rabbit on the airboat. Do you think he might get jealous?"

George sneezed.

"Yeah, probably not. It's hard to be jealous of a skinny old man in a sleeveless t and suspenders who happens to be missing three of his front teeth. Still…" Ruby grinned at herself, liking the idea that she might have someone get jealous about her.

George looked at her steadily. Did he approve? She just didn't feel well enough to figure it out.

A minute hadn't even passed when a text popped up on her phone.

Enjoying the everglades, I see. Don't let that flawless skin get ravaged by the blood sucking mosquitoes in there.

Keep heading south, Ruby. Not much further!

Ruby put the Jeep in gear and drove south. South toward Joe.

Chapter 13

It was early evening when Ruby pulled into the quiet private campground in Key Largo. She was shivering despite the Florida heat. Their campsite was on the beach with the glistening ocean behind them, but she almost didn't care.

"Maybe a mojito will make me feel better. What do you think, George?" Ruby drug herself into the camper and half-heartedly muddled the famous Cuban rum drink. Stepping outside, she sat in her camp chair and put her feet up on the fire ring. George sat in his chair next to her.

Ruby toasted her dog and sipped her drink. The usually delicious beverage tasted flat. *Damn*, she thought. *What a waste.*

George sat up in his chair and lifted both paws toward her, balancing carefully in the canvas sling chair.

"You know you can't have a mojito. What are you begging for?"

George barked.

"What?"

The dog looked pointedly at Ruby's cell phone balanced on her thigh.

"WHAT?" She was in no mood for a guessing game with the dog. She was really beginning to feel lousy.

George stood up and pawed the phone.

"You want a selfie? You want a selfie of us to send to Joe? Seriously, why the change in attitude all of the sudden?"

George sat down, posing next to Ruby.

"You're a weirdo."

Ruby composed a picture of the two of them, the ocean curving around behind them. She showed the picture to the dog and laughed as it looked like the animal scrutinized the shot.

"You really are a goof." Ruby rubbed the dog's ears and he crawled over into her lap. His warmth felt good, but the weight was irritating her. Her skin was sensitive, and her joints ached.

Absently, she sent the picture to Joe.

"George. I am crawling in bed. I feel like crap. Go potty. Hurry up."

George hopped down and did his business. Ruby picked up after her dog and they both went into the camper. She fed him and gave him fresh water then finished her mojito, brushed her teeth and turned in early.

Sometime in the middle of the night, her phone signaled a text came through. She reached over and squinted to see the lines.

Welcome to the Keys. Text me in the morning and then head south.

Ruby groaned. The text didn't bring her any joy.

George whimpered and licked her face.

"Stop." Ruby croaked. "Please, stop."

George cried softly and curled up next to his mistress.

Chapter 14

J oe lay in bed and stared at the picture of Ruby and George at the campsite. He could look at her face all night. And George's too, the damn dog. He had the curve of her jawbone memorized. He felt electricity as he remembered running his finger along that jaw before he kissed her, her lips salty from the ocean air on the beach at Assateague. It seemed so long ago that he held her in his arms, her little dog growling at him the whole time. That brought a smile to his face. That damn dog.

The dog wasn't with them the night on the dune, when Ruby had let go of some of her inhibitions, her guilt of enjoying intimacy, the guilt of a widow. Who knows how intimate they would have gotten, but the young couple who tripped over Ruby's legs in the dark and who had tumbled onto their embrace ended the mood. Everyone had laughed, embarrassed, but it had cut short the beach romantic interlude.

After that, Ruby had been hit by the jet ski, nearly died, and he had to leave the island.

Yet, she followed. It took a while, and she was not in any hurry, but she was coming. She felt the same pull he did, the same call to be together. It was just taking longer for her to accept what was meant to be. Even the dog had begun to accept the blossoming relationship.

He couldn't sleep, thinking about her. Something seemed different about her picture. He brought the text up on his phone again and studied it. Her eyes looked different. Tired. He looked closer. Her face looked swollen. She looked like she might be sick.

It was late. But she could ignore it if she wanted.

Hey, lady. Are you alright?

He waited. Nothing.

Of course, there wouldn't be a text back. It was late, and if she wasn't feeling well, she would be sleeping. He shouldn't be bothering her.

His fingers hovered over the phone. No, he wouldn't text again. What would he say? He lay in the dark, holding the phone. Willing it to bring him a message.

The screen lit up.

His phone chirped the text warning.

I'm sick.

He knew it. He knew something was wrong.

How sick are you? Are you okay?

He waited. Nothing. He was getting really anxious.

Just sick. Need sleep. Talk in the morning.

She was okay. She just had a bug. She would be okay.

He rolled over and hugged his pillow, drawing it close to him, spooning it, spooning his Ruby, trying to send comfort her way.

Chapter 15

J oe's text had awakened her. She was shivering uncontrollably, her nose running like a faucet had been turned on. She stumbled into her little bathroom, George on her heels. She blew her nose, filling the tissue completely. *Gross,* she thought. Her body was wracked with violent shivers. *What the hell? I am really sick.* George sat next to her, his eyes watching her every move. She reached for another tissue and came up with the last one.

Great. Just great. Within seconds, that tissue was soaking wet, too.

Paper towel. Ruby crossed the two steps to the kitchen and pulled a square of towel from the roll. *Ouch.* Her nose was tender, and the paper towel wasn't soft.

"Come on, George." Her voice came out in a croaking whisper. Her throat screamed in pain. "Outside and go potty."

George looked at her and hurriedly obeyed. When he came in, he didn't demand a homemade puppy biscuit from the kayak guy. He always insisted on one, but his attention was on Ruby. His lady was sick.

"I'm out of tissue, buddy. What am I going to do?" She

whispered to her dog. Back in the bathroom, she tried the toilet paper, but the RV safe paper was thin. It shredded and stuck to her sore skin.

Ruby opened the tiny cabinet over the sink. No tissues there, just a box of tampons.

Tampons.

She shivered, again. Her joints begging her to lay back down.

Tampons.

Carefully she removed one from the wrapper and gently inserted in one nostril. *That might work.* She placed the second tampon in the other nostril. Now she really was plugged up, so to speak. She smiled despite her pain. She caught her reflection in the mirror, two strings dangling on her upper lip. *Marvelous. I should send a selfie.*

Satisfied she had solved the runny nose issue, she sipped some water and crawled back in bed. She was thirsty and should have had some more water, but it was so hard to swallow with the sore throat and two tampons stuffed up her nose.

Dizzy, she fell into bed, unaware that her camper door was still slightly open. Unaware that her cell phone wasn't plugged in. Unaware of the cloud of mosquitoes that were gathering above her head.

Chapter 16

Joe woke at the crack of dawn, the pink sunrise casting a soft light over the water. This was one of his favorite times to photograph, the light so flattering. Normally he would have grabbed his camera, but today the only thing on his mind was Ruby.

He checked his phone. No texts.

It's early. If she doesn't feel well, she will still be sleeping.

He pulled a pair of shorts over his boxers and grabbed a Corona t-shirt. He and Laura had a standing date in the morning. She was an early riser and she was always grinding her coffee beans about now. Joe would join her in the morning, and they would share a quiet cup of coffee out on the porch watching the world wake up. He really liked Laura. She was feisty when she needed to be, but quiet and thoughtful at the right time. She was the best thing that had happened to his buddy Ben. When Ben had come back from service, he was lost, unsettled. Laura walked into his life and set him on a solid direction. Ben said he found a woman who understood his soul. Now they were starting a family, and his friend was content.

He wanted that for himself, too. He thought he had found his soulmate, too. It just felt right.

Joe crawled out of his teardrop just as Laura walked out on the porch with two steaming mugs of coffee. Joe smiled and thanked her as he settled into a porch rocker.

"Spill it, buddy," Laura said sternly.

"Spill what?"

"The worry that is plastered all over your face. What's going on?"

Joe grinned and handed her his phone. Showing her the picture of Ruby and the texts.

"She has a fever."

"How the hell do you know that?"

"You can see it in her eyes."

Joe peered at the picture again. Ruby's eyes had been bothering him. Now he knew why.

"Did you talk to her this morning?"

"No, I didn't want to wake her."

"I get that, but give her a call. See how she's feeling. She can always fall back asleep. When you're sick you tend not to have insomnia, even if someone wakes you up. So, put your mind at rest and call her."

Joe stared out at the ocean for a minute. Thinking about it. Laura stared him.

"Okay, you're burning a hole in my skin." Joe took a sip of coffee. "This is great by the way."

"Call her."

Joe pressed Ruby's contact information. Ruby's phone rang and rang in his ear. No one picked up. No one was answering.

"No answer?" Laura asked.

"No." Joe frowned.

You okay? He texted. He waited. Nothing.

"Call her again." Laura was quietly demanding now.

Joe didn't argue.

Ruby's phone continuously rang.

"I'll get some medicine together, and I have some home-made chicken soup in the freezer. You go get cleaned up. By the time you're ready, I'll have a get well basket ready to go."

"That's all well and good, but I don't know where she is," Joe said loudly, frustrated. Immediately, he was sorry. "Aw, Laura, forgive me. I didn't mean to yell."

Laura rested a hand on his forearm.

"No worries, Joe. I understand, and you do know where she is. She's at the Parakeet Paradise campground in Key Largo."

"How do you know that?" Joe asked, looking doubtful at Laura's psychic ability.

"Pull out that picture again." Laura insisted.

Joe brought up the picture on the phone.

"Read the sign." Laura grinned at the look on Joe's face as he saw the sign peeking into the right hand side of the picture.

"Okay, I'm an idiot. I'll take you up on the offer of the get well basket. I'm going to take a quick shower. I'll be ready in six minutes. Laura, I can't thank you enough."

Joe leaned over and planted a huge kiss on the startled Laura's forehead. She smiled happily and waddled into the house, carrying her coffee mug with her.

Ten minutes later, Joe was in his truck, Laura passing a basket full of care through the window to him.

"Tell Ben I'm sorry I won't be fishing with him today."

"Don't worry. I'll tell him you stood him up for a girl."

Joe waved as he drove away, sorry Ruby was sick, but happy he was going to go find her. See her.

Chapter 17

George whimpered at the door and looked back at Ruby. She wasn't moving. He jumped up on the bed, but she slept on.

He sniffed he strings of the tampons and sneezed.

Still nothing.

Woof.

Nothing.

He jumped down again and pawed the door. It moved slightly. He pushed with his nose. The door swung outward a foot, but moved back against his muzzle.

He jumped up on his hind legs and put his front feet against the door. It suddenly swung open and George fell face first out of the camper. The door swung closed behind him.

He regained his dignity and trotted to the small patch of grass at the back of the teardrop. He took care of his needs and sniffed around a few minutes. He was hungry, but there wasn't anything interesting at the campsite to munch on. He lifted his nose in the air and sniffed. Somewhere, he could smell bacon cooking.

His stomach growled. He was really hungry, but not

hungry enough to abandon Ruby. Sighing, he trotted back to the camper steps, then pulled up short. The door was closed.

He whined.

He couldn't get in the camper.

Woof.

Of course there was no answer from Ruby.

He scratched the door with his paw. It moved slightly. It wasn't latched, but it pushed the wrong way.

The sun was beating down on him. He was hot and hungry, and he couldn't get in. Ruby was inside. His water was inside.

He panted, drool dripping off his tongue.

He whined again and looked around him. The campers on both sides were quiet. He didn't detect any humans.

George jumped down the stairs again and circled around the camper. There was no way to get to Ruby.

It was so hot.

He came around to the front of the camper again and mounted the steps to the door. He nosed the door again. It moved inward. He tried to push his nose in the little space between the door and the frame. It just hurt his nose, and the metal was hot.

He sat on the top step and looked at the door. The sun had come up in the sky, no longer a rosy pink of dawn, but the white hot of a relentless Florida summer day. His ears slid down his head.

So hot.

So thirsty.

Woof.

George tried again. Nothing.

Whimpering, he trotted down the steps and crawled under the camper, sheltered in the shade. He could smell Ruby everywhere, but he couldn't get to her.

He rested in the shade for a few minutes, then got up to

rethink the door. At the top step he considered the crack between the door and the door frame again. He tried his nose. He sat down and looked again. He lifted his right paw and touched the door. It moved in then out. He touched it again and his toenail caught the edge of the door.

It moved outward.

He wagged his tail.

It moved inward.

He tried to curl his paw around the door. His paw slipped.

Tires crunched in the gravel behind him.

He concentrated on the door. He hooked his toenails on the door and pulled.

The door started to move, and his nails slipped off.

The sound of a truck door reached his ears.

His ears twitched.

His nose twitched.

If he could just get his nails behind the door enough, he might be able to pull without slipping.

His nose twitched again. Something… a smell…a memory.

He lifted his paw and hooked his nails.

"George?"

Startled, his nails slipped off. He turned around, frustrated.

His tail began to wag.

Joe.

George barked and turned his attention to the door again.

"What's going on buddy? Why are you out here? Where's Ruby?"

George looked up at the door again and barked.

Joe pulled the camper door open.

"Ruby?"

The trailer smelled like a sneeze.

George ran past Joe and jumped up on the bed, nosing Ruby's face.

Joe could see the shape of Ruby buried under a bulk of blankets. The camper wasn't hot, but it wasn't cold either.

George was pawing Ruby and licking her face. Ruby groaned.

Joe crossed the teardrop in three large steps and was at Ruby's side in an instant. She was curled in a fetal position, her back to him.

"Ruby?" Joe reached a hand to her and shook her gently. He leaned over and touched a hand to her cheek.

It was hot.

She groaned and rolled toward him.

He gasped and burst out laughing.

His Ruby had a tampon shoved up each nostril.

Ruby's eyes flew open.

She stared, uncomprehending. Her right hand came up, brushing her face where Joe had touched her.

Suddenly she sat up, yanking the tampons from her nose.

Joe tried to stop laughing.

She glared at him.

He sobered up quickly.

Her lip twitched.

Joe's eyes watered as he tried to stifle the mirth that was bubbling up inside of him. Ruby broke first.

The sick, feverish Ruby busted up laughing, burying her face in her hands as her nose ran freely.

Joe gave her a quick hug.

"Hang on, sweetie. I'll be right back."

Joe ran out to the truck and brought in the get well basket.

"Would this help?" asked Joe, as he handed over a box of tissue.

Ruby took them gratefully and wiped her sore nose. It was then she noticed that her face itched.

"Yeah," said Joe. "I didn't want to say anything, but it looks like a huge family reunion of the mosquito clan made a buffet of your face."

Ruby groaned and moved to crawl out of bed.

"Whoa, lady, where do you think you're going?"

"Well, unless you think all parts of my body should be leaking, you'll move so I can go to the bathroom."

Joe moved aside and helped Ruby up. She swayed on her feet. He hugged her to his side and walked her to the little closet that was the teardrop bathroom.

"Do you need help? Are you going to fall over if I let you go?"

"No," Ruby croaked. "I've got this."

She stepped in the bathroom and closed the door.

"I have to tell you," Joe called through the door. "Your old bar fly cigarette voice is very sexy. I like it."

"Ass," Ruby wheezed.

Ruby finished her business and took a minute to wash up a little. She felt gross, and she imagined she might not smell so sweet.

She couldn't believe Joe was here. How did he find her? Did she call him in the middle of the night in a fevered stupor? She didn't think so.

She stared at her reflection in the mirror. Her eyes were bright and watery with fever. Her nose red and chapped. She scratched her cheek. A mosquito bite bled slightly. All over her face were the angry red, itchy bites.

She was a disaster.

George whimpered and pawed at the door. She could hear Joe talking to him, calming him.

She desperately wanted a shower, but she really needed to lay down before she fell down. She opened the door, stumbling as she did. Joe caught her up in his arms and carried her back to bed.

He covered her up with a light blanket and brought her a glass of water.

"How long have you been sick?" asked Joe as he brushed Ruby's hair back from her face.

"It started the day before yesterday, I think," Ruby said. She furrowed her brow and tried to think back. "It started as a sore throat, and I felt achy. I guess I was getting a fever and didn't know it." Ruby paused to blow her nose. She wadded the wet tissue into her palm, not sure what to do with it. It was awkward being sick around a person you were becoming very fond of.

Joe noticed her discomfort and found a small waste container under the kitchen sink. He brought it back for Ruby. Then he went back and got Ruby a glass of water.

"Here, take these pills. It should help with the congestion and the fever. I'm guessing you'll start feeling better within the hour, unless you've taken something else?"

"No, nothing," said Ruby, as she gratefully took the offered pills and water.

"Have you eaten?"

George sat up, begging and barked.

"I didn't mean you." Joe looked at the dog.

The dog curled a lip at Joe, displaying his displeasure.

"Stop growling at me, you ungrateful cur," said Joe good naturedly.

Ruby pointed to the cupboard where she kept George's dog food. Joe poured some kibbles in the dog's dish and filled his water bowl with fresh water.

George had the decency to wag his tail in thanks.

"Now, let's try this again. When was the last time you ate?"

Ruby shrugged, fading. She was tired.

"Okay, you rest a bit. I have some frozen homemade chicken soup. It will take a while to thaw and reheat, but sleep until I have it ready."

Ruby's eyes were already closing.

"I thought you looked cute with tampons shoved up your nose," Joe whispered as he brushed his lips against her damp forehead.

Ruby reached up and lightly slapped him.

Chapter 18

J oe busied himself about in Ruby's trailer as he thawed the soup in the microwave. He found a loaf of relatively fresh bread and some slices of Havarti cheese in the refrigerator.

He buttered four slices of bread, putting two in a skillet. He topped each slice of bread with a couple slices of Havarti. The soup was thawed, so Joe found a pan and poured the soup in it to finish warming. Joe topped the sandwiches with the other two slices of bread and flipped them to brown the other side. He turned the skillet and the pan on low and went to wake up Ruby.

"Ruby, do you want to eat something?" Joe reached out and felt her forehead. She was cool. He knew it was the medicine that had brought the fever down, but he was hoping it would stay there on its own.

"Mmmm..." Ruby opened her right eye a slit. "I wish I could smell. I bet your food smells wonderful."

"Nah, you aren't missing anything. You probably won't be able to taste it either, so at least you'll be consistent."

"Where are we going to sit? I'm sleeping on my dinette."

"Do you want to sit outside? It's warm, but not too bad. There is a good breeze this morning off the ocean."

"Do you think you can pull the awning out so we can sit in the shade?"

"Your wish is my command, my dear. Hang tight."

Joe set up the awning and pulled the camp chairs underneath, making certain they were in the shade. George looked at his chair and then looked pointedly back at Joe.

"You're a real pain, you know that, brother?" George grinned at him. Joe walked to the back of his truck and pulled out his camp chair. "I'm not stupid, dog. I know my place, and I remembered my own chair."

When Joe stepped back in the teardrop, Ruby was up and dressed in a t-shirt and shorts. Her hair was pulled back in a baseball hat and her nose glistened with some petroleum jelly she found in the get well basket. She struck a pose that highlighted her nose.

"You are beautiful," Joe told her as he swatted her butt and ushered her out the door. He brought her a bowl of soup and a sandwich. "What do you want to drink, and don't say a mojito. No alcohol for you until you feel better. And speaking of alcohol, I see the evidence of a mojito in a glass in the sink."

Ruby grinned, sheepishly.

"Actually," she said, "I don't usually drink pop, but a cola sounds good. I think I have some in the fridge."

"If you don't, I have some in the cooler in my truck." Joe checked the fridge, finding it empty of cola. Once again, he made a trip to the truck, returning with two cold cans of pop.

They settled together under the awning and ate. Ruby discovered her sore throat was easing, so she was able to swallow with little discomfort.

"Do you want more?" asked Joe, when he noticed she had finished everything before he was halfway through his.

"No. I could taste it a little, and it was good, but I think I've had enough for now. Thank you." She threw the last bite of crust to George, who ate it with a smile.

"You're welcome. Actually, you're going to need to thank Laura. She's the one who fixed up the basket, and it's her homemade soup. She's one hell of a cook."

The pang of jealousy hit Ruby hard. She could feel herself deflate. George growled, deep and throaty from his chair.

"Yeah, Laura's one hell of a lady," said Joe enjoying Ruby's discomfort. She was too ill to hide it successfully. "Not only is she an amazing cook, she's beautiful, and kind, and smart on top of it all." Joe leaned back and arranged his face into a wistful stare.

Ruby felt her temper stir. She didn't think she had the energy, but look at that, it was rearing it's head, and it's fangs were sharp.

George sat up and looked on with interest.

"Perhaps you shouldn't have left her to check on me. I'm fine, so if you don't mind, you can head on back to Laura."

George licked his upper lips. He was enjoying this immensely .

Joe looked at Ruby, mildly amused.

"Oh, and she's very pregnant."

Joe waited.

Ruby's jaw dropped.

Joe grinned.

Ruby stared.

George watched.

Silence.

Then, through Ruby's hazy, congested brain, she realized Joe was messing with her. She stuck her tongue out at him and pretended to pout.

George laid down, disappointed.

"So, who is this saint?"

"Laura is the wife of my best friend, Ben. They're expecting their first child. They're my closest friends, and they can't wait to meet you. Laura would skin me alive if I didn't bring you over. They own the hotel I came here to the Keys to photograph. They also live in a small house with a big porch that faces the ocean. They have a little marina and a couple of places to park campers, complete with hook ups. That's where I'm staying and where I'm taking you."

"Taking me?" Ruby had her back up.

"Yes, taking you. You aren't well, and I want to keep an eye on you. You know you were coming this way to see me anyway, so let's just skip the games and move on. Besides, I don't think you have the energy for games right now."

Ruby thought about arguing, but realized that she just didn't have it in her.

"You look tired, honey. I think it is time for a nap. Why don't you crawl back in bed, and I'll clean up the kitchen. Then, I'm going to head to the store. I'll be back, so I'm stealing your key. I don't think you want to keep your door cracked open again like it looks like you did last night."

Ruby rubbed her face, feeling the bumps from the mosquito bites covering her skin. She couldn't believe she did that. Not only was she eaten alive, it wasn't safe. It was stupid.

"I'm not going to yell at you for not locking your door, but you need to be more careful. Please?"

Joe lifted her chin and looked into her watery eyes.

Ruby ducked her head, aware that she looked like a wreck.

"Don't. Don't ever try to hide your face from me. You're beautiful. Even when you're sick. Even when your eyes are watering, your nose is red and raw, and you have tampons stuck where they don't belong."

He got up and kissed her forehead, pulling her to her feet. George jumped down from his chair and followed.

70

Joe tucked Ruby back into bed and set about cleaning up the mess he made in her little kitchen. He checked her cupboards for staples, told George to keep an eye on Ruby, and he headed out to make sure his Ruby had what she needed.

Chapter 19

When Joe returned to the camper, Ruby was still sleeping, but her fever was still down. She stirred as she felt him lay down next to her and gather her in his arms. He tucked the top of her head under his chin and closed his eyes as he pulled her close.

George jumped on top of Joe's thigh and slid down between them. Joe opened one eye and glared at the dog. George stared steadily back. Then he wagged his tail one thump and stretched, pushing back against Joe's body.

"Great," muttered Joe, "I'm spooning a dog."

They slept together, the three of them, side by side, protecting their interests.

"Joe," Ruby whispered.

"Hmmm?"

"What are you doing?"

"Holding you and sleeping with a male dog up against my crotch. What are you doing?"

"Sleeping with dog toenails in my gut. You shouldn't be here."

"Why, you don't want me here?"

"No, because you're going to get sick. I don't want to make you sick."

"Shhh. I never get sick. It just doesn't happen."

"Yeah, right. You're some kind of super hero."

"Seriously. I really don't get sick, so don't worry. Now if George gets sick, it would serve him right. He doesn't need to be where he is."

George growled at Joe, curling his lips over his nose and baring his teeth. Then he sneezed and smiled. It was a poorly veiled warning.

"George, stop that," Ruby said as she rubbed the little dog's ears.

Joe reached a hand up and felt Ruby's face. She was cool, no longer clammy.

"How are you feeling?"

"Actually, a lot better. I think the chicken soup may have been a miracle drug, but it made me thirsty."

"Here, let me get you a glass of water. Is there anything else you need?"

"What I really need is a shower," said Ruby, wrinkling her nose.

"I can help you with that, if you like."

George jumped up and started barking at Joe, bouncing a little on his front paws.

"George," scolded Ruby. "Joe is not going to help me take a shower."

George looked satisfied.

Joe looked unhappy.

"At least not now. I'm too disgusting."

Both the dog and Joe looked at Ruby in surprise.

She must be feeling better, thought Joe.

No shit, thought George.

A startled Joe looked down at the dog. *Don't worry, fella*, he thought. *She's just messing with the both of us.*

Ruby showered and Joe ordered a pizza. When she emerged from the shower, she was able to breathe. The steam had helped to clear her sinuses, and the medicine had helped to dry her up. The heady aroma of pepperoni and onion pizza cut through what was left in her nose.

"Oh my gosh, I can smell that. It smells amazing."

They went out to the picnic table and shared the pizza, tossing the bones to George. The late afternoon light was soft, and the ocean was calm.

"I'm restless," said Ruby, fidgeting in her seat. "I'm not used to being sick either, and I feel like I've been cooped up for days. Is there anything we can do or see right now? I'm in the Keys, and I've only seen the inside of my teardrop."

"Sure, what do you want to do?"

"I don't know. Is there a place to just take a walk? Where George could go? I discovered the everglades weren't that welcoming to him."

"I have just the place, but you have to promise me that you won't overdo it. If you even start to get tired, you have to let me know. Deal?"

"Deal. What do I need?"

"Nothing except a water bottle and a leash for George. Oh, and maybe a couple of tampons for your nose."

Ruby swatted Joe, but got up and went into the camper. She stuffed a handful of tissues in her jeans pocket and pulled her Nalgene bottle out of the cupboard.

"Joe, do you need a bottle of water?"

"No, thanks, I have one in my truck. Are you ready?"

Ruby locked the camper and told George to go jump in Joe's truck.

Joe glanced over at Ruby as he drove down the road. A smile played on her lips and she swiveled her head around looking out the window. George stood on her lap, his front paws on the dashboard, tongue lolling out of the side of his mouth. George looked over at Joe and barked softly in approval.

Joe pulled into the Dagny Johnson Key Largo Hammock Botanical State Park. Ruby snapped the leash on George, and they walked over to put their park fees in the honor pay box.

"Are you sure you feel up to this?"

"Yeah. It feels good to get out."

"Okay, just promise you'll let me know if you get tired."

"I will. I will. Let's go." George pulled ahead on the leash, and they took off down the pathway into the tropical hard-wood hammock that the park is famous for.

They strolled along catching glimpses of tropical birds and beautiful butterflies. Joe reached down and slipped Ruby's hand in his. George stopped pulling at the leash and slowed to walk between them. Ruby wound up the leash so they wouldn't trip on the slack.

As they turned to follow the path to the left, George deftly turned in front of Joe, undercutting his right foot. Joe stumbled then hopped on his left foot to avoid hurting George. The dog turned back to look up at Joe as if to innocently ask what the problem was.

"Joe, are you okay?" asked Ruby as she tightened her grip in his hand, stopping his forward momentum.

"Yeah, no problem," said Joe pleasantly. *Not a nice move, dog. Don't hurt her.* George sneezed.

Not gonna happen, buddy. Just relax.

George turned around and looked at Joe.

He stared at him.

Then he lifted his leg and shot a hot stream of urine on a slim tall tuft of grass just shy of Joe's shoe.

If this is a pissing contest it's on.

"Hang on a second, Ruby."

Joe looked in both directions and unzipped his fly.

"Would you mind turning around, darling?"

Ruby colored slightly and turned her back, and Joe shot an even larger, more impressive stream of urine, bending the stalk of grass until it touched the ground.

I win.

George belched delicately and pulled on his leash, leading the way back to the truck

"I guess George is done. Ruby, how are you feeling?"

"Not bad, maybe a little tired, but the walk helped digest that pizza. This place is beautiful. Thanks for bringing me here. I can't believe how many butterflies there are."

"The Keys can be pretty magical. It's too bad you have a cold. I would love to show you the reefs."

"Why can't I see them if I have a cold?"

"You can't SCUBA dive if your sinuses are messed up. You can blow an ear drum. We can go snorkeling on a shallow reef if you want. The water is clear enough that you can see the reef even from the surface."

"I want to go, Joe. When can we?"

"Let's see how you feel tomorrow, and then we can make some plans. I can check with Ben to see if he wants to head out to Sombrero Reef. That is probably the best snorkeling in the Keys."

When they got back to the truck, Joe opened the passenger door for Ruby. George jumped in first. Joe helped Ruby up into the seat. George walked across the seat and sat in the driver's seat. He sat down watching the two of them.

Joe pushed Ruby's hair back from her face. The setting sun cast a rosy glow across her face, lighting up her raw nose. He planted a gentle kiss on her still cool forehead. Ruby smiled up into Joe's face.

George yacked up a pizza bone on Joe's driver seat.

Chapter 20

Joe pulled the truck up to Ruby's trailer. He put it in park and looked over at Ruby.

"Honey. Wake up. We're back."

Ruby had fallen asleep the moment the truck started moving.

"Hmmmm?"

"We're back. George, wake up Ruby. Go on, wake her up."

George put his front paws on Ruby's shoulders and gently licked her face and nuzzled her neck.

Ruby's eyes flew open.

"Oh George, it's you."

Joe grinned.

George growled, looking over at Joe.

That's two points for me, dog.

Joe got out of the truck and walked Ruby to the trailer. He unlocked her teardrop and opened the door for her. Ruby stepped into the trailer with George on her heels. Joe started to follow them in, but George barred the door.

He lifted his lips and shared a view of his pearly whites with Joe.

"Thanks for checking on me and taking care of me today. You were a real lifesaver. I can't thank you enough."

"My pleasure. Do you need anything else?"

"No, you've done enough. I'm just worried that you're going to get sick. I'll feel terrible."

"I told you. I don't get sick. Don't worry. How many nights did you reserve here?"

"Tonight is my last night. I have to see if I can extend my stay or find a different place."

"No, you can stay at Ben and Laura's. They already said they expect you."

"Didn't you say Laura's pregnant? I definitely don't want to get her sick. That would be bad."

"Laura is strong and used to be a nurse until they moved to the Keys and bought the hotel. I think she knows how to take care of herself."

They stood, looking at each other, Joe with an amused look on his face.

"Do you want to come in? This is silly standing here talking in the doorway."

"I would, but George is sort of in the way."

George sat down, planting himself firmly in the middle of the doorway.

"George, move, please," said Ruby.

George became deaf.

Joe leaned against the doorframe waiting. It was Ruby who was going to have to make the dog move.

"George…"

George looked up at Joe and curled his lip.

Joe smiled sweetly at the dog.

"George, move… now," said Ruby, sharply.

George's ears slid down his head, dejected. He moved from the doorway. He walked past his dish, sniffed his food, and continued to the bed. He jumped up on his pillow, curling up facing the two of them. He stared at them, daring them to make him move.

"Poor George," said Ruby. "He's out of sorts."

He's possessive, thought Joe

Because she's mine. George yawned and snuggled his nose down into his pillow.

Realizing the only place to relax and talk in the small trailer was the bed, Ruby grabbed two bottles of water and another handful of tissues and they headed outside to the camp chairs. Joe closed the camper door before George managed to jump off the bed and join them.

"Sneaky," said Ruby, fully aware of what Joe did.

Joe tapped Ruby's water bottle with his and he settled into George's chair. Ruby laughed out loud.

"Now you're getting personal."

"That I am, " said Joe as he leaned over and kissed her on the cheek. Then he wrapped her slender hand in his and held it, resting on his thigh.

They sat that way in a companionable silence as the stars came out, dotting the sky over the ocean.

"I know you have never been to the Keys before, so I need to know what you want to see and do."

"You don't have to be my tour guide. I'm sure you have some work to do."

"Actually, I don't. I finished photographing the hotel, so I decided to hang out with Ben and do some fishing for a while. I don't have an assignment for another week or so. I figure we need to go to Key West, because, well, it's Key West. We need to go snorkeling. What else, oh yeah, and Cuban Mix sandwiches. We need to get Cubans."

"I'm all about trying the food. I was so happy to get grouper up in St. Augustine. I love grouper. I think I might need more."

"How do you feel about conch? Conch chowder, conch salad, conch fritters?"

"I've never had it, but obviously, you like it." Ruby smiled at the light in Joe's eyes. The man liked good food. "But, we have to wait until I can taste things." Ruby pouted.

"It looks like you're already feeling better. The cold pills I gave you this morning should be wearing off by now, and your fever is gone. I suspect you'll need something for your nose in an hour or two."

Ruby slapped him lightly.

"How far of a drive is it for you to go back to Ben's?"

"A little over a half an hour or so. It depends on traffic."

"So, I have to leave here in the morning. Check out is early for a campground. Are you sure Ben and Laura want another trailer parked on their property?"

"I'm sure. I can drive back in the morning and you can follow me to their place, or I can give you their address and you can show up when you get there."

"Or…"

"Or…?"

"Or we can give George a heart attack, and he can sleep between us…"

"Are you sure you want to do that?"

"I don't want to do anything. I want to sleep," said Ruby.

"I didn't mean do that. I meant do that to George."

"You better not do that to George," Ruby smirked.

"You are adorable. Who's gonna break it to him?" asked Joe.

"Maybe he won't notice." Ruby stood up and stretched. She turned her back on Joe and blew her nose delicately in the tissue.

"So, that sounded like it's breaking up a bit. You can do better than that."

"I really don't need a cheering section." She hid her face and blew harder.

"Yep, my dear, it's breaking up. Laura sent some medicine for you to take at night, too. Why don't you get ready for bed, and I'll lock up the truck. I'll be in there in a minute."

Chapter 21

Ruby came out of the bathroom clad in her Ohio University t-shirt and a pair of jersey shorts. She smelled minty fresh, and her nose glistened with fresh petroleum jelly.

George was laying on his pillow staring down Joe, who was leaning against the counter in the little kitchen end of the trailer. He was pulling his boots off. When the first boot hit the floor, George growled. When the second boot followed, George barked softly. His eyes never left Joe's.

"Did you tell the dog?" Joe looked at Ruby knowing the answer.

"No, I figured he is very smart and will figure it out himself."

"I'm pretty sure he already did."

Ruby was digging in a drawer in the bathroom and didn't see the look the dog was giving Joe.

Joe saw.

Joe figured he'd better hide his shoes. He knew what George was capable of, and he could see murder in the dog's eyes.

Lighten up fella. Ruby and I are just friends sharing a space. No hanky panky...tonight.

Ruby's head emerged from the bathroom drawer.

"I thought I had a new, unused toothbrush, but I guess I don't. I'm sorry."

"No worries. I have one." Joe grinned at her as he held up a toothbrush and a travel sized toothpaste.

"Hmmm. Prepared I see."

"I wasn't sure how sick you were, and what kind of care I would need to render. Although, I can think of some ways I would like to check your temperature." Joe leered at her.

A sharp bark startled both of them.

George was standing on the bed. He was not amused...at all.

Ruby crawled into bed, a wad of tissues stuffed in her hand. Joe turned out the lights and moved to crawl in beside her. George left his pillow and stood on the side of the bed.

Move over dog. Don't make this harder on yourself than it already is.

George stood his ground.

Ruby watched amused.

I'll still be here after you are long gone. The dog moved forward, stiff-legged.

Don't bet on it, Joe glowered at the dog.

Ruby's smile faded. She felt like she was missing something, but she didn't know what.

The dog and the man stared each other down, unflinching.

Brace yourself, bucko.

Joe lifted the covers to crawl into bed. The dog rose with the comforter and tumbled toward Ruby.

"Oh, George, I'm sorry," said Joe, sweetly.

Ruby stifled a laugh, then immediately sobered at the look on her little dog's face.

"Aww, George, come here, buddy. Are you alright?" She

looked at Joe reproachfully. She scooped the dog into her arms and snuggled him to her chest.

Joe felt a twinge of guilt.

Score one for me. George looked over his back at Joe and grinned.

Ruby fell asleep with the little dog curled on her chest. In the middle of the night, she rolled over and George fit himself neatly between the two sleeping adults. He stretched his body as fully as he could to prevent them from touching. He finally fell asleep, restless and cranky.

The dog woke shortly before dawn. Ruby had moved to the far side of the bed and she was laying on her side facing Joe. Joe was laying on his side facing Ruby.

There was a space between their faces.

George had an idea. An idea only worthy of a dog like George. He crawled on his belly up toward the head of the bed. He moved slowly, carefully so as not to wake them. Once he got between the two of them, he pulled himself around so his nose was almost touching Ruby's. He stretched his back and lifted his tail. Just a little bit more. Yep, that was it.

George waited.

He was patient.

He had nothing better to do.

Except...yeah that...he was a little gassy from the pizza bones last night.

Joe was sleeping, dreaming of Ruby. He knew she was close, could feel her.

He smiled in his sleep, knowing she was near.

George smiled. Waiting.

Good morning, Joe, he thought.

Joe opened his left eye a slit. Waking up to Ruby was ...

Asshole.

Dog asshole.

"Argh." Joe jumped back and promptly fell off the bed.

Ruby jumped up.

"What's wrong? What's happening? Joe, are you alright? What are you doing on the floor?"

Joe glared at the dog. *You can kiss my ass, dog.*

You spent the night kissing mine. The dog stretched and hopped off the bed, swiping his tongue across Joe's lips as Joe still lay on the floor.

"Aww, look. He is getting used to you. He likes you," said Ruby.

George laughed all the way to the door.

"Joe, would you mind letting him out. It smells a little like he might have to go, if you know what I mean."

You little asshole. Joe got up to let the dog out. George waited patiently at the door, wagging his tail, the model of canine citizenry.

Chapter 22

"I can't believe how much better I feel."

"That is the power of Laura's chicken soup."

"I can't wait to meet her and thank her. It's like a miracle."

"Well, you'll get to meet her today." Joe whisked six eggs in a small bowl, poured them into the sizzling skillet, and stirred them into the browned ham and scallions.

Ruby worked beside him, bumping hips as she buttered three pieces of toast.

"Do you want cheese on the eggs?" asked Joe.

"Of course. Do you think I am barbaric?" Ruby smiled.

"You really are feeling better. You didn't smile much yesterday. I like this a lot better." Joe gave the eggs another stir then turned to draw Ruby into his arms. George was outside, so he took the moment to sneak a kiss and cop a feel.

"I truly am feeling a lot better. I want to kiss you, but I'm still afraid I'm contagious."

"What have I told you? Come here, you." Joe bent his head and put his lips to hers. She hesitated, but he teased her with his tongue.

"Damn, okay. If you get sick, it's your own damn fault."

"You can just take care of me."

Joe kissed her thoroughly, leaving her panting and moving up against him looking for more.

"Sweetheart, you look hungry, and I don't think it's eggs with cheese you want to consume."

"You've got that right, and if we didn't have to pull this trailer out of here in an hour, I might consider having my way with you and infecting you with all my germs."

Ruby playfully grabbed Joe's ass as she reached around him and pulled a bag of shredded cheese out of the fridge.

Joe was surprised. She had never been casual about touching him before. She always had a haunted look of guilt behind her eyes, even when it was obvious she desired him.

"Don't make promises you aren't willing to keep, sweetheart." Joe turned off the stove and backed Ruby up to the bed. She fell backward onto the comforter giggling.

George began barking as he stood on the trailer step looking through the screen.

Joe moved on top of Ruby, tickling her as she squirmed and squealed beneath him.

George started bouncing up and down on the step, barking at the door, not coming up for air.

Ruby giggled even more.

Joe pinned both of her arms over her head to the bed and pressed down on her with his body. She stilled beneath him. He transferred her hands to his left hand, still holding her down, and ran his right hand down her left wrist, his fingers trailing down the inside of her arm, then over his shoulder.

She gazed up at him, her breath coming hard.

He lazily traced the side of her left breast, moving to her nipple with a glancing brush.

She licked her upper lip with the tip of her tongue.

"Don't do that," he warned her softly.

Slowly, she reached her tongue out again to the bow of her upper lip and licked it, staring at him defiantly.

Joe groaned and crashed his mouth to hers.

George went absolutely apoplectic.

Chapter 23

"Joe, the eggs are getting cold."

"That's the only thing that's cold, honey."

"George is making too much noise. Someone is going to come."

"No kidding, you're right. Someone is going to come."

"Joe, seriously," Ruby pushed back against him, regretfully.

"Buzz kill." Joe stood up, laughing, pulling Ruby up with him.

They stood together for a moment, holding each other. George stopped barking. He sat looking through the screen at them, growling softly.

Joe traced the line of her jaw with the backs of his fingers, brushing her lips with his thumb.

"One of these days, we're going to finish what we start. I promise you that."

Not if I can help it. The dog barked sharply.

"Joe, George wants in. He can probably smell the toast. He knows I always make him one when I make one for me. He loves toast."

He's going to be toast if he keeps interrupting me.

Joe walked over to let George in. George smiled as he walked past Joe then neatly yacked up some grass onto the tip of Joe's shoe.

"Oh, I'm sorry," said Ruby. "He's been spitting up a lot lately. I hope he's okay."

"I'm sure he's fine. He did that with the pizza bones last night. Maybe we shouldn't be feeding him people food. Maybe we shouldn't give him that toast."

Don't even think it. George moved closer to Ruby and sat up, putting on his most adorable begging face.

Then stop blowing chunks on my stuff. Got it, buddy? Joe took the toast from Ruby and tore a piece off.

George's eyes narrowed.

Joe handed him the bite of toast.

George took it politely.

"Good dog," said Joe as he patted Ruby's butt, grinning.

They sat at the picnic table, finishing breakfast and sharing small bites with the docile dog. When they were finished, Ruby secured everything in the teardrop while Joe washed the dishes and put them away in the cupboard.

George watched the activity from his pillow.

Joe checked the hitch, making sure everything was in order for Ruby to tow.

"Okay, you're just going to follow me. It should only take about forty minutes to get to Ben and Laura's. If you need anything, just call, okay?"

"Joe, I have been pulling this trailer without your help up until now. I'm certain I can follow you without a problem." Ruby looked a little miffed.

George liked that.

He decided to look miffed, too. He curled his lips up.

Bad move, bucko. You just keep doing that. George wagged his tail and smiled sweetly and Joe.

"Okay. Let's go." Joe reached in the window and scratched

George's ears for a second. The dog stretched his neck out. It felt so good, and he couldn't help himself.

Yeah, Ruby feels the same way when I do that.

George snapped, his teeth clicking together.

"George, what has gotten into you?" Ruby yelled.

"I think there was a fly or something bothering him," said Joe, looking steadily at the dog.

Sorry. George licked Joe's hand briefly.

Me, too buddy. I was out of line.

Chapter 24

R uby expertly backed the trailer onto the trailer pad next to Joe's teardrop. She put the Wrangler in park and set the brake. George was hopping up and down in the seat, looking out the window, his tail wagging. There were a flock of birds on the ground nearby that needed to be scattered.

Ruby opened the door and George streaked out, barking with glee as the birds took flight.

"George. Come here. You need to behave. We're guests here."

A musical laugh met Ruby's ears as she turned to see an extremely pregnant woman coming toward her. Joe intercepted and gave Laura a big hug, then let her go, appraising her condition.

"No offense, woman, but you've gotten bigger since yesterday." Joe teased, and Laura swatted him on the arm, but was grinning just the same.

"Joe, that's horrible. Hi, I'm Ruby and I apologize for Joe's insensitivity. He's obviously an oaf of a man who needs new filters installed."

Laura just laughed again and gave Ruby an unexpected hug.

"Welcome to Pelican's Roost. I'm glad you're here, and I'm thrilled you've put a smile on Joe's face."

Ruby blushed and returned the hug.

"Thank you for the basket filled with healing. I can't believe how much better I feel. I swear your chicken soup is some kind of miracle drug. Have you considered packaging it and selling it?"

"You're very welcome, and I don't have the energy to do that. Especially now. I've become very lazy." Laura patted her stomach lovingly.

"If I may ask, when are you due?" Ruby eyed the large round bulge that Laura was carrying in the front. "You kind of look like you're going to burst."

"Two weeks left, and I feel like I'm going to burst. Do you have any children?" Laura asked.

A look of sadness shadowed Ruby's face. George moved over to his mistress and reared up on his hind legs, hugging her with his front paws.

"No, I never was able to conceive."

"Oh, I am so sorry, Ruby. I didn't mean to pry." Laura's compassion touched Ruby's heart.

"It's okay. I came to accept it, but my husband, he never did. He wanted a family so badly."

George whimpered softly, pawing Ruby. She bent down and picked him up, hugging him to her chest.

Joe stood by quietly.

I am so sorry, buddy.

The dog ignored him and cuddled with Ruby.

Laura broke the awkward moment by reaching a tentative hand toward the dog.

"I absolutely love this dog. What is he?"

"A Border Terrier mix," Ruby responded.

George wiggled around in Ruby's arms until he was facing Laura.

He appraised her.

She waited patiently.

He melted.

Squirming, he let Ruby know he wanted to be put down. Ruby obliged. George walked over to Laura and politely sat, raising his paw in greeting.

"I would love to shake your paw, little guy, but I'm afraid I can't bend over that far." She patted her belly in apology.

George stretched up on his hind legs and carefully balanced his front paws on her thighs. Laura scratched his ears with delight.

"I always wanted a dog and was never able to have one. Maybe someday. Well, I'll leave you to get settled. Ruby, make yourselves at home. You're welcome to anything you see here, and if you need something and don't see it, please feel free to ask. Ben should be back in a couple of hours. Would you guys join us on the back deck for dinner tonight?"

Ruby and Joe looked at each other, questioning, but not comfortable enough with each other to answer for the other. It was so obvious that they both wanted to do it, but didn't speak that Laura laughed again.

"I'll take that as a yes."

"We don't want to be a burden, " said Ruby hurriedly. "Please tell me how I can help or what I can bring."

"You aren't a burden. I won't lift a finger. I make Ben and Joe man the grill. No worries. I will see you guys later."

With that Laura turned and walked to the house. After a moment's hesitation, George trotted after her.

"I think George just fell in love," said Joe, amused.

"No kidding. What's up with that?" Ruby asked, surprised at the fact that her buddy and protector left her side.

"Ya wanna take advantage of it?" Joe said, wagging his eyebrows.

"Yes, but no. This is the first time George has left us alone voluntarily. I don't want to betray his trust."

Joe looked at Ruby incredulously.

"Please tell me you are kidding."

"Yes, and no. Yes about George, but what I want to do is find a grocery store so I can contribute to dinner tonight. I showed up without a hostess gift, and I will not show up to dinner empty handed. Capeesh?"

"Yeah, I get it, but Laura and Ben are very laid back."

"Understood, but I was brought up with manners. Am I going to unhook my Jeep from the teardrop now, or are you going to drive me somewhere so I can go shopping?"

Ruby put both hands on her hips, her right toe tapping.

"Yes, ma'am. Your wish is my command. We need to go and get George."

Ruby whistled for her dog.

She whistled again.

A minute later, George came running to her, full tilt, his ears flapping in the breeze.

Chapter 25

R uby sat in a lounge chair next to Laura. Between them was a small table with an array of cheeses, meats, and crackers that Ruby and Joe brought with them. Laura sipped on a virgin mojito that that Ruby created. Ruby was drinking the real deal, and the men were nursing some craft IPAs from a local brewery.

George was laying under Laura's lounge chair munching on a new bone Joe bought him, and Reggae music was playing softly in the background. Ruby sighed. She could stay here forever.

George stopped chewing and looked up at her. His lady looked content. Happy. Relaxed. He glanced over at Joe. Joe was watching Ruby over the rim of his bottle as he took a sip.

I'm going to have to stop giving Joe a hard time. The dog yawned.

Yes. Yes, you are. But I understand if you slip now and then.

George smiled at Joe as their eyes met. Then he raised his upper lip as a reminder who was boss.

Joe raised his bottle in salute.

"Are you proposing a toast, Joe?" Laura asked.

Joe colored slightly.

Laura glanced down at the dog whose head was peeking out from under her chair.

"Yes, I am. To old friends, new friends, and cranky friends."

They all took a sip.

"Who the hell is cranky?" asked Ben.

"George." The others all said at once.

George thumped his tail sheepishly.

O ver dinner of grilled spiny lobster tail and small sirloin steaks garnished with garlic butter, they talked about what Ruby should see in the next couple of days she was there to visit. Ben offered their scooters to Joe and Ruby to take to Key West if they wanted.

"Have you ever ridden a scooter, Ruby?" asked Joe, concerned.

"In college, I had a roommate who had one. I rode it around some, but it's been years. I assume it's like riding a bike, you never forget. I'm more worried about the fact that I don't have a license."

"It's the Keys," laughed Ben. "No one will care if you go slow and don't draw attention to yourself."

"Live dangerously while I'm down here, huh?"

"Sure, why not," said Joe. "If something bad happens, you can always write an article about how not to get arrested while vacationing in the Florida Keys."

"Now that's an article I would like to read," said Laura.

"I also want to take Ruby snorkeling, if possible."

"We could go out to Sombrero Reef if you want," said Ben.

"That's exactly what I was thinking," said Joe.

Ben pulled out his phone to check the upcoming marine forecast. Ruby noticed that Laura was especially quiet.

"I'm going with you guys," said Laura softly.

"What?" said Joe, protectively.

Joe noticed Ben hadn't heard her.

"I said I'm going snorkeling, too. Sombrero Reef is one of the best places in the Keys to snorkel, and I want to watch Ruby as she gets to see it for the first time. Plus, I haven't been snorkeling in ages." Laura pouted.

"But you're pregnant," Joe sputtered.

"Really? I hadn't noticed."

"No, I mean you're really pregnant. Like I'm afraid to be around you pregnant."

Ruby laughed and choked, spewing mojito on the deck. George jumped up, helping to clean up the delicious drink.

"George stop. That's not good for you." Ruby casually shooed George away, then slipped him a piece of cheese to go with his beverage.

"Ben, aren't you going to say something? Are you going to let her go?" Joe pleaded with his friend.

"Let her go? Oh Lord. Look out." Ben pretended to duck for cover.

Laura's back was up.

George hid behind Ruby.

"First of all, I'm not sick, I'm pregnant. Second of all, there is no need to be afraid of me. Third, I'm a nurse, so I know what I can and can't do. Fourth, floating in water is good for me. It will take some of the pressure off my back for a while and feel good. Fifth, I am smart enough to not put myself or my baby in danger, and sixth and last, I am going to enjoy the hell out of watching you squirm the whole time, mister." By the time she was done talking she had moved closer to Joe and was poking her finger in her chest.

George was howling with delight.

George loved Laura.

I love you, too, George.

The dog wagged his tail, happily.

I t was late when they all said goodnight. It was decided that Joe and Ruby would take the scooters to Key West in the morning. The marine forecast predicted the waves to be lower the following day, so they were planning on snorkeling then, Laura included.

Laura offered to watch George for them when they went to Key West, and George seemed comfortable with the decision. At least that's what Laura told Ruby and Joe. Ben just looked at her like the pregnancy may have made her a little crazy.

Ruby and Joe said goodnight and went into their separate trailers.

George was comfortable with that, too.

Chapter 26

"Come on George, hop up." Ruby patted the seat in front of her.

"What do you think you're doing?" asked Joe, watching with interest.

"I feel bad for leaving him all day, so I want to give him a ride first. I think he'll like it."

"Dogs don't ride scooters."

"Yes, they do," said Ruby stubbornly. "I had a cousin who had a dog that would sit on the motorcycle seat and put her paws on the gas tank. My cousin would sit behind her and off they would go. She would ride that way both on and off road. There used to be a YouTube video of that dog trail riding. Ziggy loved to ride."

"Okay, what the hell, give it a shot."

"Come on, George. Up."

George hesitated for a minute, then jumped up on the seat. He shook and teetered, and he turned and tried to find the right position to get comfortable and feel stable. Ruby arranged him to her satisfaction, then started the scooter.

George trembled.

Ruby scratched his ears, then put the scooter in gear.

Damn it, she is nuts. The dog spread his front paws apart a little further to help brace himself.

She might be, but we love her for it.

George looked sharply at Joe.

Joe looked surprised himself.

There wasn't time to contemplate the thought because Ruby took off with George hanging on for dear life. She buzzed down the lane and turned toward the road.

Laura stepped off the porch and walked over to Joe, watching her scooter disappear around the corner.

"She's special," Laura mused.

"I hope you mean that in a good way," Joe chuckled.

"I most certainly do. She has brought light back to your face, and I will be forever grateful for that."

"Yeah. Maybe she has."

"The dog is special, too, but you know that, don't you?" Laura searched Joe's eyes.

"Yes, I'm afraid I do."

"It's important that you don't hurt her, Joe."

The sound of the scooter reached their ears. Ruby was on her way back. George was sitting comfortably, his nose in the air, ears flapping, lips puffing out with the wind. He was thoroughly enjoying himself.

"Seriously, Joe, try not to hurt her, " Laura repeated, "or the dog just might kill you."

No shit, thought Joe.

No shit, smiled the dog.

Oh, shit, thought Laura, as she shook her head.

L aura stood on the front porch with George beside her. They watched as Ruby and Joe headed out on their day trip.

"Come on, George. I bet you would like a puppy biscuit."

George looked up at her and happily wagged his tail.

They went into the house together and Laura curled up on the couch with a book. George sat and looked at her. She patted the couch next to her, inviting George up. He smiled and gently jumped up, curling around her very pregnant stomach. He laid his nose gently on her abdomen and listened to the sounds of life inside her. He sighed wistfully and squinted his eyes.

I'm sorry, my friend. Laura scratched the top of the dog's head as he lay with his muzzle cocked sideways, his ear pressed against her belly.

George fell asleep and Laura read her book. She lazily ran her fingertips on top of her stomach, cooing to her baby as she read. The baby stirred in her belly.

George opened his eyes.

The baby kicked George in the head.

George wagged his tail happily and looked up at Laura with adoring eyes.

Chapter 27

Ruby and Joe rode the scooters southwest, along the oversees highway, crossing bridges over sparkling blue water. They stopped when they felt like it to take in the scenery. At one point they grabbed some Cuban coffee from a small market. Another time they treated themselves to a slice of key lime pie.

The sun was hot, but the ocean breeze was fresh. Joe reminded Ruby to reapply sunscreen every time they hopped off the bikes and two hours after they started, they pulled the scooters into Key West.

Ruby squealed with delight at the houses crowded together painted in candy colors. She posed for a picture in front of the oldest and largest banyan tree in Key West, and they waited in line to stand at the southernmost tip of the United States.

"Are you hungry and ready for some lunch?" Joe asked her when they parked the scooters so they could explore the city on foot.

"Yeah, I could use some food. Where are we going? Hemingway's Hideaway? Or an overpriced, commercialized island theme restaurant? I am game for any of it. I am loving acting like a tourist."

"We're going to a laundromat."

"Wait, what?"

"You heard me."

"We're going to a laundromat for lunch?"

"Trust me," said Joe.

Ruby shrugged and fell in beside him. As they walked, Joe reached over and snagged her hand, holding it carefully in his.

He stopped them in front of a long building. There were benches outside with people sitting on them reading the newspaper, laundry baskets parked at their feet. On the right side of the building were windows revealing rows of washing machines. The windows on the left side revealed a small room with tables and a tv on the wall. In the middle of the building in front of the benches was an order window and some outdoor stools pulled up to a counter.

"Good morning," Joe said to the smiling women behind the order window. "Could we get two Cuban sandwiches and two colas, please?"

"Wait," said Ruby.

The woman stopped, her pencil held in the air. She and Joe looked at Ruby expectantly.

"Um, what's on a Cuban sandwich?"

The lady smiled and shook her head, looking at Joe.

Joe shrugged at the woman and held up one finger to her, telling her to wait.

"So, there is a hot debate as to what goes on a Cuban, but these have ham, marinated shredded roast port, Swiss cheese, mustard and dill pickles all hot pressed on crusty Cuban bread. Is that okay?"

"It sounds perfectly wonderful, except for the mustard. Can it not have mustard?"

"Not authentic that way, but for you, no mustard."

The lady bobbed her head and hurried away with their order. Ruby and Joe settled onto stools at the counter and watched the activity on the street.

"Joe look, that chicken is just walking down the street. Did someone lose their chicken?"

"Haven't you noticed any of the chickens yet?"

"No, just this one, why? Wait there's another one. Isn't that a rooster or something?"

"They are called gypsy chickens. They roam free and are actually protected. They are from when the Cubans worked in the cigar factories that were here in Key West. The workers brought their prize chickens from Cuba with them when they came here for work. They used to fight them. Terrible business, but when the factories closed, the chickens were left. The fighting cocks bred with the regular chickens that were left behind, and now the city has a population of chickens that roam around. Wait until we walk around downtown. You'll find them wandering into the open air bars and markets. It's all part of the charm of Key West."

Their sandwiches arrived accompanied by a basket of hot, golden fries. Joe waited as Ruby tasted her sandwich. A look of pure satisfaction crossed her face.

"Good?"

"Amazing. The flavor is so full. The roasted pork is delicious, but this bread…this bread is out of this world."

"It would have been better with mustard," Joe teased, looking at her sideways, his mouth full of the sandwich.

They stuffed themselves, then left a large tip and headed on foot for the hopping part of downtown Key West.

Chapter 28

The sun was hanging low in the sky, and Ruby and Joe worked their way down the sidewalk to Mallory Square Dock for the sunset festival. After a day of shopping, sightseeing, and adult beverage consuming, they were mellowed and moving slowly. The pink-tinged clouds lit the sky over the water, and the soft light warmed the landscape. Joe backed Ruby up against a low wall and photographed her with her face washed in the warm pink sun rays. Then he moved her against the concrete dock and photographed her silhouette with the setting sun behind her. Normally awkward about getting her picture taken, Joe made her feel comfortable and even a little sexy.

They held hands as they watched a sword swallower and an acrobatic act, and ate conch fritters as dusk began to settle on the key.

Walking back down the sidewalk under the tropical vegetation, Joe pulled Ruby into his arms. Island music played from the porch of a large Bahamian home, and Joe and Ruby slowly danced in the street to the sultry Reggae tune, steel drums moving their feet in rhythm.

Ruby sighed, her head resting against Joe's shoulder.

"I don't want tonight to end. This day has been amazing."

"It doesn't have to. We can dance on this street forever if you want. There is nothing stopping you."

A car approached, it's lights shining on the dancing couple. Instead of the angry honks that Ruby braced herself for, the car slowed and drove in a wide arc around them. The face of an old Cuban man leaned out the window.

"Love her, mon. Love her until the day breaks and the shadows flee."

Joe and Ruby smiled and waved, still swaying under the palm fronds.

Then Joe took Ruby's hand and led her up the wide steps of the gracious island house. A couple sat in a wicker porch swing sharing a cocktail, their voices a soft murmur.

"What…?"

"Shhh…" Joe's index finger touched Ruby's lips.

"Do you want the night to end, or would you like to stay in this island fairy tale until morning?"

"Stay."

Joe opened the door of the home and led Ruby to a big antique roll top desk that graced the wide open front hall. The house was cool and fresh. Stained glass pineapples decorated the high window transoms. Hardwood floors gleamed with a soft glow, and the light smell of beeswax, coconut, and citrus scented the air.

Ruby wandered over to the window to look out on the porch, drawn by the street lights filtering through the intricately cut pineapple wooden gingerbread that decorated the porch, while Joe checked in with the hostess.

Then he took her by the hand and led her up wide ornate stairs and slipped the key into the door at the end of the hall.

Ruby smiled up shyly at Joe and he pulled her into his arms as he nudged the door closed with his foot.

"Is this okay with you," he asked her as he nuzzled her hair.

"Yes," said Ruby, her voice husky. "Um, what about George?"

"Don't worry, we won't hear him growling over here."

Ruby laughed and pulled away, studying Joe's face.

"Seriously. What about George? And when did you plan this?"

Joe took both of Ruby's hands in his and gazed at her earnestly.

"I didn't plan this. Laura texted me and told me if we were tired and it was getting late, she had made arrangements for us to stay here. The proprietor is a friend of hers and they had a vacancy. Laura said George hasn't left her side. I told her that your trailer was unlocked and where George's food is. So, if you want, we can spend the night here together. If you don't, we can go home."

"I do," whispered Ruby.

"Also, we don't have to do anything you don't want. I have no expectations other than to enjoy my time with you."

Ruby dropped Joe's hands and reached up placing a palm on each side of his face. She looked at him steadily, clearly.

"I want to."

Joe bent his head and brought his lips to hers. He kissed her softly, carefully. Ruby returned the kiss. She flicked her tongue against his lips, and he opened them to allow her to explore.

He splayed his fingers into her hair, gathering the glorious locks into his hand and gently pulled her head back exposing her neck. He bowed to it and ravished her throat, tasting the saltiness of the day. She moaned and leaned back, allowing him to gain access to the front of her shirt, which he quickly unbuttoned. He slipped his hand inside her shirt and palmed her breast, feeling the nipple harden beneath him.

Ruby's breath hitched and came faster. Suddenly, she couldn't wait any more. There had been too much time, too much pain, too much sadness. A wildness broke inside her, and she tore at Joe's shirt clawing to reach his skin, his solid, hard chest. He obliged her by pulling off his shirt and sliding hers to the floor. In an instant her bra lay beside her blouse and their chests were together, their hearts echoing each other.

In one smooth movement, Joe swept Ruby into his arms and carried her to the high, antique mahogany button four poster bed. He eased her back and flicked the button on her capris. She moaned in anticipation. He slid her pants off and hooked his fingers into her panties.

She was panting in impatience, wild with hunger. She reached for his jeans, but he moved her hands away. He swung her legs onto the bed and moved beside her, kissing her deeply. She responded, writhing beside him. He worked her nipples as she pressed herself to him, then he reached for the v in her thighs and brought her to a crashing climax.

She cried out, her release complete.

Joe didn't stop. He worked her, kissing her deeply, moving his hands to her breasts, teasing her again. She mewed against his lips, the yearnings coming again in a strong wave.

This time she was insistent. Ruby reached down and stripped Joe of his jeans, dragging his boxers with them. She rolled Joe on top of her and found him hard and ready. She lifted her hips to his and they came together in a dizzying frenzy, crying out together and collapsing as one.

Chapter 29

R uby woke to Joe tracing the outline of her lips. She smiled, and he kissed her eyelids, her nose, her lips. They had made love two more times during the night, each time a new exploration of each other, a new discovery.

"Good morning." Joe smiled down at her.

"Good morning." Ruby covered her mouth with her hand.

"What's wrong?"

"I'm sure I have morning breath."

"Never! Your breath is sweet as gardenias in the morning."

"Well, aren't you the poet, and I think you might be fibbing a bit. I need a toothbrush."

"There's a new one on the counter in the bathroom, just waiting for your pearly whites."

"You smell remarkable minty fresh," Ruby accused Joe.

"I may have slipped out of bed earlier and used one of the toothbrushes. I vaguely remember doing that. Vaguely."

Joe trailed his fingers down Ruby's back as she got out of bed and walked to the bathroom. Despite the quaint, antique theme of the room, the bathroom had all modern appointments.

She found the unopened toothbrush, and she cleaned her teeth. On the counter was a basket filled with handmade soaps crafted in the Keys. She picked up one of the silky bars.

Ruby turned on the shower and stepped into the steamy deluge of water. She soaped her body with the bar of coconut and jasmine soap, breathing in the scent of the island.

The curtain slid to the side and Joe slipped in behind her. He lathered her shoulders and back working his hands down to her hips. Rich bubbles sparkled against her freckled skin. He pulled her soapy body against his, her back against his chest, her bottom cradling his penis. His hand circled her, soaping her clavicles, lathering her breasts. Ruby's hands reached for the wall, steadying herself as the water cascaded down on them.

Chapter 30

R uby and Joe rounded the corner, pulling into the lane. George leaped off the deck, chasing the scooters until they parked by the back shed. Ruby jumped off the bike and crouched down. George threw himself in her arms. He jumped and barked and licked her until she fell onto the ground where he continued to cover her in kisses. She laughed, hugging him to her, scratching his ears whenever he held still enough for her.

"Hello, George," Joe said, reaching down to give the dog a pet. He stopped just short of touching him when he caught the look in George's eyes.

I'll deal with you later. The dog raised his lips at Joe then turned his attention back to his lady.

Laura waddled up to them, watching the joy between Ruby and George.

"He missed her," Laura told Joe.

"No doubt," Joe replied. "Did he give you a hard time last night?"

"Not at all. He was a perfect gentleman. It wasn't until he

heard the scooters that he started to get antsy. Did you have a good night?" Laura looked at him slyly.

"I don't kiss and tell," quipped Joe.

"I think you owe me a little of the story, don't you?" Laura pried.

"Probably. I can't thank you enough. That was a brilliant move on your part. Sneaking little bitch, aren't you?" Joe looked lovingly at his dear friend.

"Yeah, I was bored, and I think you guys needed a little push in the matchmaking area."

"Well, I'm not sure of that, but you sure helped make a great evening even better. Is snorkeling today still on?"

"Yep, Ben is getting the boat ready, and I have packed the cooler with some drinks and snacks. We have plenty of masks, fins, and snorkels in the shed. Why don't you and Ruby change into swim suits and pick out some gear that fits."

Ruby got off the ground, brushing the sand from her capris.

"Hi. Thanks for watching George and arranging the bed and breakfast last night. That was very thoughtful." Ruby blushed as she spoke the words. Laura kindly ignored Ruby's discomfort.

"Do you need any help with that cooler, or getting anything ready?" asked Ruby, noticing that Laura looked a little tired.

"Nope, everything is ready to go. It's not much, just some light snacks and drinks. Go get changed, and we'll meet you down by the dock. I figured George can come. Is that alright with you?"

"Absolutely. He has his own lifejacket. He wears it when we go kayaking.

"Perfect. Ready in thirty minutes?"

Ruby and Joe went into their trailers to change, George never leaving Ruby's side. Ruby emerged wearing a teal bikini top and matching board shorts. She carried a beach towel and

George's life jacket. Joe met her outside her teardrop, and they walked to the shed and picked out snorkel gear.

As they walked to the marina, they caught up with Laura who was lugging the cooler.

"What the hell are you doing?" Joe scolded Laura. "You shouldn't be carrying that." He took the cooler from her, and Ruby relieved Laura of her tote bag.

"Damn guys, I am not an invalid."

"No one thinks you are, but we want to be able to snorkel. We don't want to be delivering a baby on a boat instead," said Joe looking a little nervous.

Ben helped Laura and Ruby onto the boat, and Joe helped to cast off. They settled themselves in for the short boat ride to Sombrero Reef.

When they arrived, they were able to tie off to an empty buoy. Within minutes they were ready to go in the water.

Joe and Ben steadied Laura as she moved to the swim platform and put her fins on. She slid into the water and stretched out, a huge smile on her face.

"This feels so amazing. Pregnancy and buoyancy go together well." She swam away a short distance to make room for everyone else to get in the water.

Ruby got in next, admonishing George to be a good dog and keep an eye on the boat. He barked and wagged his tail, then jumped into the captain's seat so he could get a bird's eye view of the snorkelers.

Once everyone was in the water, Ben and Laura led the way. Laura stayed on the surface, while Joe and Ruby dove down and skimmed along the reef looking at the amazing amount of bright colored reef fish. Ben divided his time between floating lazily with his wife and diving below to share the reef with his friends.

Ruby kicked her feet up executing a perfect surface dive that drove her eighteen feet below the surface. Joe appeared next to her, and they skimmed along the trench that bordered the reef.

Ruby grabbed Joe's hand and excitedly pointed off to her left. A green sea turtle swam lazily by them. They watched as long as they could before they had to swim upwards for air.

Ruby gasped as she broke the surface.

"Did you see that? That was amazing!" She gulped air into her deprived lungs.

"Yeah, that was pretty cool. Are you okay?"

"Okay? Yeah, I'm okay. Let's go."

Ruby sucked in a lungful of air and dove again, looking for the turtle. She was not disappointed. She swam alongside the creature, enjoying its graceful, effortless movements.

A few seconds later, Joe grabbed her hand and drug her upwards.

"What's wrong?"

"Nothing, but we've been out here awhile. Laura and Ben are already on the boat. I don't want to be out here too long, because I think Laura might be tired."

"Oh my gosh, I didn't think of that. I'm so sorry."

"There's nothing to be sorry about. They didn't signal us to come in. It looks like she's drinking some water and petting George. If Ben needed us, he would have signaled, but let's head back anyway. Is it okay? Have you had enough?"

"I don't think I will ever have enough, but enough for today. I'll race you back to the boat."

With a flick of her fin, Ruby shot forward, Joe in quick pursuit.

Chapter 31

Ruby and Joe joined Laura and Ben on the back deck later that evening. Joe and Ruby had gone for takeout for all of them, and they spent the evening relaxing in each other's company. Ben and Joe made plans to go fishing in the morning. Laura swore she was going to spend the day on the couch.

"Ruby, do you want to go fishing with us?" asked Ben. "I'm sure Joe won't mind baiting your hook."

"I can bait my own hook, you chauvinist pig," Ruby teased. "But I'm worn out, playing too hard. I think I need a down day, plus I just checked my email and my inbox is full of editing jobs. I have a deadline coming up fast for "Better Breast Butters", and "Snacks that Make You Feel Sexy", right behind it."

Ben stared at Ruby, his jaw dropped.

"Please tell me you're kidding."

"I wish I were. You can't believe the stuff I have to edit. I can't tell you how many articles about semen I've had to correct."

"What can you write about semen?" asked Ben, shaking his head.

"Artificial insemination of race horses, the benefits of semen on the skin, I could go on and on, but by the look on your faces, I don't think I should." Ruby was laughing at their expressions and decided to go for the jugular. "It's better than the herpes articles. Is it just a skin rash, or is it herpes?"

"Oh, no, please stop," moaned Ben.

"Well, feel free to work on the deck or in the house tomorrow if you want. I seriously am going to hang out on the couch and read, and I would love the company," said Laura.

"You really want George's company," accused Ben. "She's smitten with that dog. I'm afraid when you leave, not only am I going to be a new daddy to my very own baby, but I think there might be a dog in the house soon, too."

Laura just smiled a secret smile and excused herself. She begged off the rest of the evening saying she needed to rest.

"Is Laura okay?" asked Joe.

"Yeah, I just think she overdid it today. I didn't think it was a great idea for her to go snorkeling, but I wasn't going to tell her no. She's smart, and I have to trust her. But the day really wore her out. I'm going to follow her and turn it, too. Feel free to stay out here as long as you want. I'll see you guys in the morning." Ben left the two of them and George out on the deck. They sat in silence watching the night sky until the wee hours of the night. Then they walked back to their trailers and said goodnight, parting ways for the night.

Chapter 32

Joe knocked on Ruby's teardrop door. She emerged holding a steaming cup of coffee, her hair glistening, still wet from the shower.

"Good morning, gentlemen," She smiled at Joe and Ben. George pushed his nose past her legs, appraising Joe.

"Good morning, Ruby," said Joe, as he leaned past the dog to give her a kiss. "We're heading out now, okay? It's going to be a while before we get back."

"The fish we're going for today are in deep water," said Ben "so it will take us some time to get to our fishing spot. Laura is still in bed. She's tired, and her back is sore today. Would you mind keeping an eye on her?"

Ruby nodded her head, looking concerned.

"Of course I don't mind. Is she okay?"

"Sure. Just tired. The baby is due in two weeks, so she tires easily. She did a lot yesterday, and it's catching up to her."

"Ben, we don't have to go fishing. We can stay here. I'm fine with that," Joe's worry showed clearly on his face.

"No, Laura told me to go. I think she wants some peace and quiet. She told me that she'll have Ruby here if she needs anything, and she's just going to sleep and read, so we'll be fine. Ruby, make yourself at home here."

Ben turned to leave, and Joe took a moment to pull Ruby into his arms. George stood stoically by her side.

"I'll miss you today. I got spoiled these last couple of days," Joe murmured as he stroked her damp hair, trailing his hand down her back.

"I'll miss you, too, but I do have a lot of work to do. Catch some big fish, then come home to tell me lies about the ones that got away."

"No lies for you lady. I will tell you the sorry truth, even if it kills me." He kissed her lightly and turned to follow Ben.

No need to hurry back. George stretched beside Ruby, bowing to the floor with a groan.

Love you, too, George. Joe turned and waved goodbye to the two of them.

Ruby gathered her laptop and supplies and slipped her feet into her favorite flip flops. She picked up her coffee and looked down at George.

"You ready to go hang out on the deck with me?"

George wagged his tail happily. He was glad to have his Ruby to himself.

Ruby settled herself at the umbrella table and tried to work, but found herself distracted by her surroundings. It was so beautiful here. Vibrant magenta bougainvillea climbed the posts of the deck, and hummingbirds darted around eating nectar from Laura's garden. A parakeet landed in a nearby tree, it's green feathers flashing in the sun.

"George, I have to get to work, but I just want to sit and soak this all in."

George jumped up on Ruby's lap and swiped his tongue across her chin. He settled down, groaning in pleasure as she rubbed his ears and the top of his head. Ruby's laptop sat, untouched.

A minute later, George's tail started thumping. Ruby looked down and saw George looking over his shoulder. His body quivered in anticipation.

"What's going on, George?" Ruby asked, then smiled as she saw Laura coming through the patio door. The smile was immediately replaced with a look of concern.

"Laura, are you okay?" Ruby stood to go over to her, dumping George off her lap onto the floor.

Laura smiled, tiredly.

"Yeah. I'm just tired, and my back hurts today. Nothing awful, just a dull ache."

"Why don't you sit down, and let me get you something. How about some hot tea?"

"You are my guest. You don't have to wait on me."

"I'm no longer your guest. I'm your friend, so can I get you that tea?"

"Yes, that would be wonderful. There's some decaf in the tin by the electric kettle."

"Don't worry. I've got this. Are you hungry?"

"No, not really, but thanks."

Laura settled onto the wicker couch, propping herself up with some pillows, but no matter what she did, she just couldn't get comfortable.

George looked on anxiously sensing that Laura was in distress. He didn't know what to do, so he sat down and offered her a paw.

Laura laughed.

"You look like a worried papa. I'm fine little guy."

George stood back up and paced, feeling unsettled and anxious. His tail wagged when Ruby came through the door with a tray of tea and some scones she found in a bakery bag on the counter with a note beside the bag from Ben.

She placed the tray on the low table in front of Laura and handed her the note.

Laura read it and smiled.

"Ben knows I adore snickerdoodle scones. He is such a worrier. He left you instructions on how to contact him with the marine radio if I need anything. I had to move heaven and earth to get him to go today."

"Joe was okay with not going. I think he feels bad about taking Ben from you now. He looked kind of miserable when he left."

"Ruby, I made Ben go. He has been hovering over me for days now, and I can't breathe. I needed some time without that. I know that sounds bitchy, but I just needed some space. Do you know what I mean?"

"Yes, I do. I like having Joe around." Ruby stopped at Laura's raised eyebrow. "Okay, the truth be known, I love having Joe around, but I need space for myself. I need time to figure out me and what I need and want."

"You do like Joe a lot, though right?" Laura's protective side was rising to the occasion.

Ruby laughed, watching Laura's countenance turn, ready to fight for her friend.

"Yes, I like Joe…a lot…a whole lot, but I want to be careful. I don't ever want to hurt him. I became single unexpectedly, suddenly. I didn't welcome it. I didn't want it. I loved my husband." George whined and pawed Ruby. She lowered herself into a chair and allowed George on her lap.

"I'm sorry, Ruby. I am so sorry that your husband died," said Laura, her face riddled with compassion.

"Thank you," Ruby whispered, her eyes glistening with tears.

"Ruby, I'm guessing your husband loved you very much. Joe told us the story of what happened and how you got your teardrop. That is as romantic as hell and heartbreaking." Laura glanced at George. The dog looked steadily into her eyes. His tongue licked his lips. "The thing is, he loved you unconditionally. He loved you enough to give you a symbol of freedom. With that came the blessing to love again."

Go on. George sneezed quietly.

"So, take a chance on love. Don't walk away from it because you feel guilt or a duty to your husband who has passed. I think your husband would be sad if he thought that had happened."

Ruby thought for a moment before she spoke. Laura and George waited.

"I know all of these things. Intellectually, I know that my husband is gone, and I have a wonderful life ahead of me still to live. But sometimes I feel he is watching me, and it hurts him that I have feelings for someone else."

See, I told you. Laura stared pointedly at George.

George licked his paw, ignoring her.

George, don't ignore me.

He looked at Laura and yawned.

"Of course, your husband is watching you. He's in a good place, and I believe he's cheering you on. I imagine it would be hard for a man to see his wife love another, but a man who truly loved his wife would want her to be happy. I am certain your husband truly loves you, and although he wishes he could be by your side, he would be grateful that you found someone who could love you and protect you for the rest of your life, and you found someone who you love with all the passion you have inside of you."

Ruby smiled faintly as she thought of the night she and Joe had spent in the bed and breakfast. It was magical.

Shit. George jumped off Ruby's lap.

Exactly. Laura watched as the dog trotted off the porch to relieve himself.

Chapter 33

R uby worked steadily, plowing through the skin care and snacks. Her editor had sent her two more articles to work on with the admonishment not to work too hard and to enjoy her time on the road. Ruby sent the two articles back with a personal note to Laney, letting her know that she was fine and soaking up the sun in the Keys.

Laura slept soundly on the couch, the ocean breeze lifting her hair. George rested by Laura's side on the floor. Ruby was half way through the third article, "Ingrown Toenails are Not Your Friend", when George whimpered and stood up, looking at Laura anxiously. Ruby glanced over and noticed the sheen of sweat on Laura's face.

She walked over and looked down at her new friend. George glanced up at Ruby's face and then looked at Laura and whined. Laura seemed to be sleeping soundly, so Ruby walked into the house. She pulled a pitcher of iced tea out of the fridge and filled two glasses with ice. She came back out on the deck and poured herself some tea. With the sound of tea pouring over the ice cubes, Laura stirred.

George reared up and placed his front paws carefully on

the couch. Looking intently into Laura's face he flicked his tongue out to graze her chin. Her eyes slid open.

"Hello, George."

"I'm sorry he woke you up, Laura."

"That's okay. Is that iced tea over there?"

"Yep, I brought you a glass. Would you like some?"

"Yes, please." Laura lifted herself up, scooting so she was sitting with her legs still stretched out. She scooched her butt sideways, trying to get her back to stop hurting. The pain moved in waves. One minute she was feeling better, the next her back throbbed and ached.

"Laura, are you okay? Are you too warm? Can I get you anything?"

"No, thanks, honey. This iced tea is hitting the spot."

Laura sipped the tea and absently scratched George's back. He moved so her fingers scratched the base of his tail. He moaned as he stretched his nose to the sky, relishing in Laura's attention.

Laura set her tea down and closed her eyes. Within minutes, she was sleeping again. Ruby watched her for a minute then turned her attention back to the laptop.

Ruby worked steadily for another hour and was in the middle of writing her own article about her day in Key West and snorkeling on Sombrero Reef. As she was describing the encounter with the sea turtle, her thoughts were interrupted by Laura crying out and George whining with distress. Laura moved off the couch holding her back, looking bewildered.

"Laura, what's wrong? Honey, what is it?"

Laura shook her head, trying to clear the sleep, when her body was wracked with a searing pain. She nearly fell to her knees. Ruby was by her side in a second, steadying her.

"Ruby, could you please help me to the bathroom. I seem to have some trouble standing."

George paced, whining softly, sitting, then standing, and pacing again.

Ruby slipped her arm around Laura and steadied her, walking her through the patio door and down the hall to the bathroom.

"Do you need help in there, or would you like some privacy?"

"I think I've got this." Laura closed the door.

Ruby paced anxiously.

"Laura honey. Are you okay? Can you please tell me what's wrong?"

"I'm good. It's okay." Laura's voice sounded like she was gritting her teeth.

Ruby pulled her cell phone out of her pocket and tried to call Joe. There was no answer. He was probably too far off shore to get any service. She texted him for good measure. *Call me, please. It's important.*

Ruby heard the toilet flush and the sound of Laura washing her hands. The door opened, and a very pale woman emerged.

"Laura," Ruby gasped. "What's going on?"

"My water broke." Laura gasped in pain. "And I'm in active labor with my contractions about a minute apart. I'm pretty sure I'm going to have this baby. Like now."

Ruby wrapped her arms around Laura. She was terrified. Laura looked scared, but the look on George's face was laughable.

Ruby pointed at the terror stricken dog, and Laura burst out laughing.

"I think poor George is going to faint," said Laura.

"He might not be the only one," murmured Ruby. "Okay, what do you need me to do?" she asked after taking a deep breath.

"Could you please get me to my bed? On the way, I want

you to go to the linen closet…" Laura paused to deal with the next contraction. Ruby waited, supporting her friend. "Okay, so get the red and white checked plastic tablecloth out of the closet and a bunch of beach towels." They paused by the closet and Ruby loaded up on the supplies. Then they made their way to the bedroom, pausing each time Laura needed to gather herself. George faithfully stayed by Laura's side.

Ruby spread the tablecloth on the bed followed by a couple of layers of towels. Laura climbed in and tried to make herself comfortable.

"Laura, shouldn't I call 911 or something?"

"Ruby, I'm not dying. I'm having a baby."

"Okay, but this isn't a hospital, and I'm not a doctor. I don't think I'm the kind of person you want to have yanking a baby out of you."

"Ruby, please, whatever you do, don't yank."

Laura cried out, then panted, breathing through the pain.

"Oh shit, Laura, please let me call 911."

"Ruby, this baby is going to be born before an ambulance can get here."

George yelped and ran from the bedroom.

Ruby remembered the marine radio.

"Laura, can I use that radio and call Ben? Will it reach him?"

"Yes, but we don't want to panic him. We will just tell him that he needs to head home."

"Laura, he needs to know that you're in labor."

Pain seized Laura, and she gasped forgetting to breathe. Ruby saw the panic start behind Laura's eyes, and she realized that she needed to step up and take charge, but she had no idea what to do.

Chapter 34

B en slid the boat into the slip, coming in hot. He leapt from the deck and ran down the dock toward the house. Joe tied the boat to the cleats, making certain the bumpers were where they belonged to protect the boat, then he hurried after Ben, not knowing what to expect, but worried about Laura and Ruby.

When he reached the house, he found George pacing back and forth in the living room. An ambulance was parked in the driveway, and Laura's cries could be heard echoing through the house.

"Hey, buddy," said Joe.

George turned and looked at Joe, wagging his tail nervously.

"Ya wanna go outside for a walk?" Joe offered, anxious to get out of the house.

George hesitated, looking back toward the bedroom. Laura cried out again and George came running for Joe.

They escaped outside, where they both found themselves pacing.

A few minutes later, Ruby stepped out of the house, pale and exhausted.

Joe and George looked up at her, holding their collective breaths.

Ruby smiled, and it was radiant.

Joe whooped and ran for her, lifting her into the air, swinging her, kissing her.

George jumped and barked, happiness sounding with each yip.

"What the hell happened?" asked Joe, as he came up for air.

"Laura and Ben had a baby," Ruby said simply.

"Yeah. I gathered that, but wasn't the baby supposed to wait two more weeks? What the hell happened?"

"I guess the baby was impatient." Ruby laughed with relief.

"Are they okay? The baby and Laura, are they okay?"

"Yep. They're just fine. They had a beautiful baby boy." Ruby wiped the tears from her eyes.

"Hey, what's wrong? Why the tears?" Joe brushed her cheek with his thumb, moving the tears aside.

"I was so scared."

"I'm sorry, but it looks like you did okay."

"Okay? She did great." Ben swept Ruby into his arms and hugged her tightly. "Thank you for taking care of Laura and Joey. I am so sorry I wasn't here, but thank you for being there for her."

"No problem. Thank God the paramedics arrived right before he came out. I don't know if I could have done it alone. I was so afraid of dropping him."

"Wait, you delivered the baby?" asked Joe, astonished.

"Yes, she did. The paramedics coached her through it. She was already doing it when they came, so they just made sure everything went as it should."

"Sir, are you ready to go?"

"Go, Ben, where are you going? Is everything okay?"

"Relax, Joe. Laura and the baby are going to the hospital to get checked out. No worries." Ben clapped his hand on his friend's back and followed the paramedics out.

George ran after Ben, catching up with the stretcher that carried Laura and the baby. He went to jump up on the bed, but a young blonde paramedic grabbed him.

"Whoa dog, what do you think you are doing?"

"Let him go," demanded Laura, not unkindly.

"I can't let him jump up on here."

"Why not? What's going to happen?"

"Well, it's not sanitary, for one thing."

"This baby is going to be fine. George germs will not hurt him."

Ben picked up the happy dog and held him so he could give Laura a look and gaze upon the baby.

The dog whimpered and quivered with delight. He adored the small, pink human being.

Chapter 35

L aura and Joey came home the next day. Ruby had already cleaned the bedroom, washing all the sheets, comforter, and towels. She had a pot roast braising in a Dutch oven on the stove surrounded by onions, potatoes, and carrots, and she had baked two loaves of Italian bread.

Joe took care of things around the hotel and marina, making sure everything was done so Ben could spend time with Laura and Joey. And when Ben brought his family home, Ruby, Joe and George made themselves scarce.

They kayaked through the mangroves searching for manatees, George standing in the front of Ruby's kayak looking in the water and barking at fish.

As they glided together through the water, their paddles pulling them forward silently, Ruby broached a subject she had been dreading.

"Joe, I'm going to have to be leaving." She stopped paddling and looked at him.

"I know."

"You know?"

"Of course. Ben and Laura need to have time alone as a

new family, and I'm guessing you have a job to do. At the very least, you must be itching to continue your adventure, exploring the country in your teardrop."

"What about you?"

"That depends."

"On what?"

"Where you are going?"

"Why, are you stalking me?" Ruby laughed.

"No, just letting you know I'm not interested in having you drive out of my life. So where are you heading?"

"Laney asked if I wanted to head up to Monongahela National Forest in West Virginia to do a story. The travel magazine wants something about a climbing spot called Seneca Rocks and an area called Dolly Sods. I figured I'm game."

"Hmmm. I would love to get some good pictures of climbers. When are we going?"

"Are you serious?"

"If you don't mind a tag along. I promise I'll give you space and not expect you to spend every minute with me. I will respect your need to write, your personal space, and even your time alone with your dog."

George pulled his attention from looking for fish and turned to growl at Joe, but it was only half-hearted. Then he wagged his tail.

"I guess we're traveling in a caravan of teardrops. When will you be ready to go?"

"Let's check with Ben and Laura and see if they need any help, then head out. Day after tomorrow?"

"If it's okay with them, then let's do that. I think I'm going to like having you tag along."

"I think I'm going to like stalking you."

George gave a warning growl.

I was talking about stalking you, George. Joe thought.

You're a lousy liar. George yawned, then barked excitedly as he spotted the graceful shape of a manatee gliding beside the kayak.

That evening, Ben walked over to Ruby and Joe's teardrops.

"Hey guys. Someone made an amazing pot roast that we would love to share. Please join us on the deck. Please don't keep hiding from us. We had a baby, not leprosy."

Ruby laughed and put her hand on Ben's forearm.

"We just wanted to respect your time together. That's all."

"Well, we want you to get to know lil' Joe. Will you come?"

Joe looked at Ruby. She smiled and nodded.

George sat up and begged. He was not going to miss the time with the baby.

They spent a quiet evening eating Ruby's pot roast and holding the baby. George made sure he was posted by the baby each time he was passed to the next person. George was Joey's sentry, his guardian. George was filled with joy when he was near that child.

Chapter 36

Two days later, Joe and Ruby had their teardrops hitched to their vehicles, and they were saying their goodbyes to Ben and Laura with promises to stay in touch and exchange pictures.

Joe kissed his namesake on the forehead, and honorary Auntie Ruby gave him a stuffed dog that looked a lot like George.

Laura and Ruby hugged. Through tears, Laura thanked Ruby again for being there and reminded her that no matter what happened between her and Joe, Ruby was always welcome, she was now family.

Ruby motioned for George to hop into the front seat of the Jeep so they could get moving.

George didn't move.

He just sat and stared at Lil' Joe.

"George, hop up into the Jeep."

George looked back at Ruby and whined, then looked back at the baby.

Come on, George. Go with Ruby. Joe whistled for the dog.

Torn, the dog stood. Hesitated.

Come on, George. Ruby needs you and loves you.

George ran to Laura and reared up on his hind legs, gently resting his front paws on her thighs. He reached up his muzzle to sniff the baby. Laura obliged, dipping down so George could nuzzle Joey.

George stayed a minute. Looking up at the tiny baby. He whined softly and flicked out a small, pink tongue.

Then he jumped down and turned. He looked into Ruby's eyes and smiled a big, fat doggy smile.

Then came running.

He sailed through the air and landed in the front seat ready to go for a ride.

They pulled out of the gravel lane and turned onto Highway One, heading back toward mainland Florida. Joe was leading the way, and Ruby followed, marveling at how tiny his teardrop looked behind his truck. She would chuckle when she passed the big RV's and the driver would look astonished at the size of her tiny trailer. The driver didn't realize what he was missing. The size of Ruby's trailer required her to do most of her living outside. Sure, she could cook in the trailer, but she preferred to use the little propane grill she carried or to cook over the campfire. Often, she would use a Dutch oven. She didn't always like to heat up her little trailer or send grease flying into the air.

The folks that traveled in the large trailers were surrounded by luxury, sure, but Ruby felt that they were missing out. They stayed inside most of the time, not enjoying the great outdoors. What was the point of camping then, she thought.

On the other hand, she was glad to see the older folks when she was traveling. Most of the time they were friendly and accommodating. It would be hard on some people who had mobility issues to move around in her tiny trailer, especially if they had to turn the bed into a dinette every day. And Joe's trailer only had a bed. Someone with a bad hip or back might have a rough time performing the required gyrations just to pull on a pair of pants in a teardrop.

"I guess whatever it takes to follow your dream and travel, huh George?"

George looked at her with his happy dog smile and barked in agreement. When they pulled out of Ben and Laura's, George was mopey, but after they had put a hundred miles under their belt and George had a good nap, he was back to his old self.

"Hey Joe," Ruby spoke into her cell, "I think George needs to go outside, and I could use a potty break myself. Would you mind stopping pretty soon?"

"I was just thinking about a cup of coffee. Does that fit the bill?"

They agreed to pull over for coffee and a leg stretch and within minutes, Joe had found an independent coffee shop. Ruby took George for a walk while Joe went in and got them coffee and a snack.

They sat outside on the shaded patio and enjoyed their break. George lay comfortably between Ruby's feet watching some children playing at a nearby playground.

If only. George sighed.

Joe slipped a bit of his danish to the dog under the table.

George took it gratefully, but still raised his lip in a tiny snarl.

It's okay buddy. You have to keep up appearances. Joe flipped him another piece.

That night they rolled into a small private campground near the freeway.

Joe grilled a couple of steaks over the campfire, and Ruby made a salad and some aglio e olio pasta with red pepper flakes as a side. They sat and watched the fire dance, enjoying the peace and stillness of the evening. When the mosquitoes made it uncomfortable to stay outside, they each went their separate ways into their trailers to finish up their day's work and get some rest for the next day's travels.

They settled into a steady rhythm. Both were early risers and quick to get ready in the morning. Ruby wasn't high maintenance, and Joe was relaxed but motivated to get moving after they had coffee together. They were relaxed with each other, and George was becoming more accepting of Joe's constant presence.

They weren't in a hurry to get to Monongahela National Forest, so they only traveled about six hours a day, stopping to see the sights that intrigued them. Only a few hours away from West Virginia, Joe called Ruby.

"Let's pull over for something to drink and some lunch."

Ruby followed him off the freeway. Joe drove into a small town and parked his trailer on the street near an old diner. Ruby found a place a block away. When she stepped out of the Jeep, Joe was waiting for her.

"I'm afraid George is going to have to wait in the trailer. The diner isn't dog friendly."

"It's okay. He's used to it."

George looked disgusted but hopped into the teardrop and curled on his pillow to wait for his people to come back.

Nice choice for a stopover. I expect something good from this. George sneezed into his pillow.

"I'll steal a piece of bread or roll for you buddy. Don't you worry," said Joe.

"Joe, you know he isn't supposed to get people food. Why do you tell him that?"

"A piece of bread won't hurt him, and I have to keep him on my good side so he doesn't growl when I want to kiss you."

Joe demonstrated.

George growled.

Thank you.

You're welcome.

146

Chapter 37

"Are you sure you're okay with me going?" Joe had broken the news to Ruby that he had to make a side trip in order to photograph a hotel in Virginia. Ben had a friend who was excited about having Joe do the same kind of work for him and had called Joe, insistent that he would make it worth Joe's while to alter his plans.

"Joe, don't be ridiculous. We both have a job to do. We aren't bound to each other, we're just traveling together and hanging out. I like having you around, but if you're gone for a couple of days, it's not a worry."

Joe pulled her hand into his from across the table and squeezed it warmly.

"I know we've only known each other for a short while, but I have grown accustomed to having you around. I like you, Ruby. A lot. I don't know where this is going to go, but for now, I like you in my life. It's important to me that you're okay with me going to get this job done. This is just a rest stop. That's all. I'll come back."

Ruby laughed warmly. It was nice having someone want her, need to be with her, but he didn't feel like he was drowning her. She thought it was awfully cute the way he was looking at her with his puppy dog face, worried she was going to be mad, but concerned that maybe she didn't care. If she was another kind of woman, she would have enjoyed and exploited the power.

"Okay, you'll be gone, what, two days max? It's only a half days drive from here, plus you need to wait for good light to take the pictures, so two maybe three days. I'll get a spot and reserve one for you next to me. I'll check out the area and figure out what we might want to do. Then I will laze around and catch up on my own work. No worries, Easy peasy."

Joe looked doubtful for a minute, then smiled.

"You always amaze me. I have to remind myself you are nothing like my ex-fiancée. I can't begin to tell you what this would have been like. I would have you go with me, but I know you have an appointment to interview that climbing instructor, and you said he leaves for Utah soon. I don't want you to miss him."

"Joe. It. Is. Okay. Unless you are taking pictures of a hotel for your ex-fiancée, I don't care."

"Hot damn. So, you would care if it was her place? We're getting somewhere. You like me."

"Yes, Joe. I like you. Now stop acting like a goof and eat your burger. George gets cranky if I ignore him for too long."

They finished eating, splitting the bill between them. Joe pocketed a piece of leftover bun he had saved and a couple of crackers for George. He walked Ruby to her Jeep.

"Okay, you know how to get where you're going, right?" Make sure you go slow and gear down in the mountains. Go slow around curves, and if someone behind you gets antsy, just ignore them. They can wait."

Ruby stared at Joe, amusement and slight annoyance lighting her eyes.

"Joe, I managed just fine before you came along. I'm sure I can manage just fine now."

"Have you ever trailered through the mountains?"

"Yes, well, no. Foothills. I'll be fine. Gear down. Go slow. Got it."

"Call me when you get in. Please let me know you're safe."

"Same as," said Ruby. This time she initiated it. She pulled Joe to her and kissed him.

George's mouth dropped open. He forgot to pant.

Joe laughed.

"What? My kissing you is funny?" Ruby looked pissed.

"No, your dog is funny."

Ruby looked at George, who tried to look innocent, but didn't quite succeed. Ruby laughed and lightly kissed Joe again.

"Safe travels. I'll see you in a couple of days. Give George the food you have hidden in your pocket and George, get in the Jeep."

George stepped up to Joe with dignity. Joe presented the dog with his snacks. George sniffed them, just to be sure.

Seriously? You think I would poison you?

George smirked then delicately devoured the food.

Thanks. George turned his back to Joe and farted as he jumped into the front seat of the Jeep.

Chapter 38

R uby rolled into the National Forest campground near Seneca Rocks. She was astounded to see that the campground was nearly full. A ranger told her that the campground was at near capacity because of a large family reunion nearby. He said he had only been here for a short time, had never seen anything like it. He suggested a site in the back, not very level, but is was open.

"I guess we'll give it a shot, George. I hope there is a place for Joe when he shows up."

George smiled at the thought of Joe's possible misfortune.

Ruby followed the one-way signs until she came to the site the ranger had suggested. She wouldn't have electricity, but that didn't bother her. She was eager to use her boon docking solar set-up. She was considering wintering on Bureau of Land Management land out west, and she would need to be adept at using her solar setup in order to stay out there for a month at a time.

Ruby expertly backed her trailer in to her spot. It definitely wasn't level. She pulled out a few small boards she carried and rolled one trailer tire onto the stack. She grinned. It was pretty cool that her trailer was so small she could push it around herself. Satisfied the trailer was level enough, she blocked the wheels and set about making herself at home. There were no empty campsites nearby for Joe anywhere. She certainly hoped someone would clear out before he came.

Maybe she should just try to reserve one for him. Or at least let him know.

She tried to call him, but there wasn't any answer. Instead, she texted him that she was safe and set up. Then she suggested he try to make a reservation for when he thought he would show up. She waited for a return text, but none came.

She was surprised that bothered her.

An old beat-up Jeep pulled into the site next to hers. A ratty pop-up trailer was already occupying the site.

A well-muscled man with long blond hair hopped out and grinned at her, giving her a lazy wave.

Ruby waved back and smiled. She loved how friendly everyone was when camping.

George did not smile.

George did not wave back.

"Be nice," Ruby warned.

George vocalized his dissent, chewing the growl for effect.

"You are a goof." Ruby rubbed the dog's ears and he groaned. "I was expecting Joe to eat with us tonight. I have the stuff to make a batch of jambalaya, but there will be too much for just me. On the other hand, I don't have anything else to make. I supposed I can save the leftovers for lunch tomorrow," she told the dog conversationally.

Ruby pulled her Dutch oven out of the back of her Jeep and started a wood fire and lit some charcoal. Once the charcoal was ready and the Dutch oven sitting over it was hot, Ruby browned slices of Andouille sausage until each piece was crispy on the outside, but still moist and tender on the inside. Then she added some vegetables, rice, spices, crushed tomatoes, and broth, and set the lid on the pot. She added coals to the lid and let the mixture cook. Satisfied, Ruby went into the trailer to make herself a mojito, thinking this was turning out to be an okay day.

Ruby emerged with a tall, refreshing drink and a book. She spun the lid on the Dutch oven a quarter turn and the body of the oven a quarter turn in the opposite direction. Then she settled into her camp chair and stretched her feet toward the fire. Situated as she was, she could gaze at the rock pinnacles of Seneca Rocks looming above her.

The jambalaya bubbled gently beside her, and George sat in her lap. Her book lay on George's chair. Ruby realized she hadn't had a moment to herself in that last week. She wasn't sure how she felt about that. She missed Joe, but she did enjoy this relaxed peace.

The man in the next campsite came out of his camper and put a little backpacking camp stove on his picnic table. He put a small pot on the stove and added a pouch of food and water. He stirred it and added a lid.

Ruby picked up her book and started reading, glancing up occasionally to look at the mountains and watch her good-looking neighbor.

He went back into his camper.

George stood up on Ruby's lap and growled, his hackles raised. Ruby looked in the direction George was staring. A squirrel was hopping across the picnic table heading toward the neighbor's little backpacking stove.

George barked.

The man came out of the camper.

The squirrel jumped into the camp stove, knocking the pot off, and spilling the man's dinner.

"That was not cool." The man stared at his dinner. He half-heartedly tried to scoop it back into his pot. It was futile.

Ruby got up from her chair and wandered over to the man's campsite.

"Sorry about your dinner."

"No worries. I have some granola bars."

"Would you like to share some of my jambalaya? I have plenty, actually more than plenty. Do you like spicy food?"

"I don't want to impose."

"You're not. My name is Ruby, and that is George."

George did what George always did. He lifted his lip in a snarl.

"Your dog doesn't want to share."

"Don't worry. He'll get over it. I just have to add the shrimp and let it cook for a few more minutes."

"Okay, I'll grab my plate and a spoon, and I'm Micky."

"Nice to meet you, Micky, and you don't need to do that. I have plenty."

George jumped up into his camp chair laying claim to his space despite the book beneath him. Micky walked to his campsite and picked up his camp stool while Ruby went into her teardrop and got the shrimp out of the refrigerator.

Using the sturdy metal hook, Ruby carefully lifted the lid of the Dutch oven. The air was filled with the spicy aroma of the Southern dish. She stirred the shrimp in and it immediately began to turn pink. She popped the lid back on and went back in the camper to get a couple of plates and utensils.

"Do you need something to drink?" Ruby asked Micky from the camper kitchen.

"No, thank you. I have some water. That's pretty much all I drink. Can I help you with anything?"

"Nope, I have everything. We can eat at my picnic table if you want."

Micky took the plates from Ruby as she stepped out of the camper, and he waited respectfully as she spooned jambalaya on each plate.

"Please, sit down." She waved him to the picnic table.

George jumped down from his chair and sat next to Ruby on the bench of the picnic table. He divided his attention between Ruby's plate and staring down Micky.

George did not like Micky.

"This is delicious," said Micky, as he dug in.

"Thank you," Ruby mumbled, her mouth full.

It was quiet for a few minutes as they enjoyed the spicy dish. Ruby offered Micky seconds, and he happily accepted. When they were finished, Micky picked up his plate and offered to help with the dishes.

George growled at him and blocked the way into the camper.

"What's with the dog?" he asked Ruby, as he passed his plate through the door to her so she could wash the dishes in the camper.

"He is very protective. He doesn't really like men."

As if to make the point perfectly clear, George growled again.

"That's just not cool, man," Micky said to the dog.

George didn't care what Micky thought.

Micky wandered over and added some wood to the fire. Ruby emerged from the camper a few minutes later. She watched Micky, his back to her, as he poked the fire, encouraging the flames to catch the new wood.

He was incredibly attractive in the cover of a romance novel kind of way. His longish hair gave him a boyish look. His thin frame was layered in hard muscles, the black t-shirt accentuating his form. His moves were graceful, and she could imagine him climbing, his strong fingers searching for cracks in the rocks, his strong forearms picking up his body.

George looked at her sideways. *What the heck? What about Joe? What is she thinking?* He squinted at her, willing her to look at him.

155

Ruby glanced at her dog. George was so tense. He needed to learn to relax.

"So, are you here to climb?" Ruby asked Micky as she settled into her camp chair near the fire. George jumped into his chair after Ruby moved the book she had neglected.

"Actually, I'm here for a family reunion, along with most of the other people in this campground. Once a year the entire clan meets here to celebrate marriages, births, and deaths, not necessarily in that order."

"That sounds like fun," said Ruby, "or not." The look on Micky's face gave her a clue to his feelings about the fun of it all.

"I try to hang by myself most of the time, and I climb when I get the chance, but my granny lays on a mighty big guilt trip if I stay away too much."

"Granny. You really call your grandmother granny?"

"Yes, because it pisses her off. She says it makes her sound ancient."

"Are you climbing tomorrow? I would love to watch if I could. I'm here because I'm doing a story about the climbing scene here."

"Sure, you can tag along, if you want. I'm going in the early morning though, before the sun gets too hot. It'll be boring after a while. You can only watch so much of someone moving slowly up a rock."

"I can amuse myself. I don't want to intrude, but I might come and watch for a little while."

"Do you hike?"

"Sure."

"If you get bored there's a great trail that takes you up to the top of the rocks. It's a heck of a lot easier to go that way than to go my way. Plus, you can take your dog with you."

"That sounds good."

"I'll be leaving around six in the morning, if you want to join me. Bring plenty of water for the trail."

With that Micky said goodnight. He picked up his chair and thanked Ruby again for the food.

He ignored George.

George ignored him.

Before Ruby went to sleep, she tried to text Joe again, but there was no signal. Feeling a little unsettled, she snuggled down in bed, but had trouble getting comfortable. George groused about her tossing and turning. Finally, after an hour of restlessness, Ruby fell into a fitful sleep, feeling like her world just wasn't right.

Chapter 39

Ruby dressed quickly in the morning, tying on her hiking boots and pulling a yellow bandanna around her unruly hair. She packed a backpack with some granola bars, cell phone charger, and a couple of bottles of water. She added some puppy biscuits for George and his collapsible water dish. As a last-minute thought, she rummaged in her cupboard until she found a tea bag for cold brew tea. She would have to forgo coffee this morning, and she didn't want to develop a caffeine headache. She could put the large teabag in her Nalgene bottle and have lukewarm tea in an hour or so. That would stave off the withdrawal symptoms.

As she locked up her trailer, Micky was emerging from his, carrying a pack full of climbing gear. He had his hair caught back in a pony tail, and he looked carefree and unconventional.

Ruby loved it.

George did not.

"Are you ready?" Micky asked.

"Just let me grab my hiking poles out of the back of my Jeep. My knees aren't happy if I hike without them."

Micky waited patiently for her, then the three of them took off, walking toward Seneca Rocks.

Ruby hung out of the way as Micky set up for his climb. She jotted notes and watched quietly, hoping to remember some of what Micky did to reference when she interviewed the instructor at the climbing school.

Within minutes, Micky was climbing gracefully up the rocks. It was like a slow dance. Micky reached his hand carefully and hooked his fingers on a hold. He stretched his leg, reaching out with his toe looking for the perfect place. Then, when he looked like he was in an impossible situation, he worked his muscles, and his body followed a path into a new, stable position. Sometimes he moved upwards, other times sideways. Always slow and deliberate.

George yawned.

He was bored with the whole thing.

Ruby kind of liked watching the man move up the cliff, the muscles in his forearms, back and legs rippling with every move. It was kind of hot.

Joe, you'd better get your ass back here. George whined softly.

There was no reception.

After watching for an hour, Ruby was ready to move on. Her neck was getting a crick in it, and Micky had moved high enough that it was harder to see what he was doing. She supposed it was pretty exciting to do the actual climbing, but she had to admit, Micky was right, it wasn't much of a spectator sport.

"You ready to go for that hike, George?"

George jumped up, his tail wagging. He was very definitely ready to go.

They crossed a river in the beginning of the hike then

proceeded though a deep forest on a wide trail with a gentle incline. Soon, they reached a set of steps which they easily conquered. They climbed steadily through a canopy of trees, the trail switching back regularly to make the ascent easier. After climbing for a while, they stopped and sat on a downed tree, taking a minute to eat granola bars and puppy biscuits. Then Ruby drank her tea and shared some water with George, who lapped it down happily.

She checked her cell phone for the umpteenth time this morning, but there still wasn't any service. She was completely unconnected from Joe and her editor. She wasn't very happy about that.

"George, I'm spoiled. We never used to have cell phones or be constantly connected. It's crazy that I'm so dependent on this damn thing." With that she decided to stop carrying it in her pocket and throw it into her backpack. She wasn't going to bother with it for the rest of the hike.

After the one-mile mark, the trail grew even more rocky, and Ruby could tell they were near the summit. As they rounded a corner, she caught a glimpse of a large deck built to jut out over the cliffs. The view looked like it was going to be amazing.

"Come on George. Let's go look."

George put his front paws on the platform and stopped.

"What's the matter, buddy?" Ruby looked down at her little dog and was surprised to see his ears flat against his head and his tail between his legs.

"Come on, let's take a look at this crazy view."

George wouldn't budge. Ruby bent down to pick him up and realized he was shaking. She hugged him against her chest and stepped onto the platform, walking toward the railing.

Ruby was right. The view was breathtaking.

George was having none of it.

He turned in her arms and wrapped both front paws

around her neck. His back toenails dug into her belly, and his muzzle was pressed against her shoulder, buried under her hair.

"Oh no. You're afraid of heights, aren't you? You poor thing." Just like my husband, Ruby thought. I could never get him to look over the edge.

Ruby took George off the platform and then tied his leash to a tree a safe distance from the edge of the cliffs. She walked back to the platform and enjoyed the panoramic views of the valley. George sat stoically watching her. She turned and started back to her dog when she noticed the trail went higher onto the rocks, leading to the top of the mountain. There was a huge sign cautioning people to think twice before going beyond the sign. The notice cautioned that the trail beyond was only a few feet wide, and a running tally of the number of people who had died was featured prominently.

George barked at Ruby.

She looked back at him and grinned.

She was on her own. No one could tell her to stop.

She could do whatever she wanted.

Take risks.

She wanted to.

George stood up. He growled.

"Stay here George. I'll be right back."

George whined and tried to look pathetic and cute.

Ruby laughed.

"I'll be back. Don't worry." With that Ruby started up the rocks, holding on and carefully placing her feet, testing her balance, and moving upward.

George paced on his short leash.

Ruby looked back and smiled reassuringly.

She decided that looking over her shoulder wasn't a wise move because it shifted her balance.

George whined and paced.

Ruby moved upward, climbing cautiously, feeling freer with each step closer to the top. The rock surface narrowed, and Ruby was truly on the crest of the world. The mountain dropped straight down on both sides of her, and she was standing on a knife edge of rock. It was exhilarating. It was dizzying.

"It's stupid to be up here without proper gear." The disembodied voice startled Ruby.

"Excuse me?"

"If the rock gave way, you'd fall to your death." A head popped around a rock and a girl climber smiled at Ruby. "I'm not trying to be an ass, but I don't want to see you fall. Please be careful. You're not tied off to any ropes. Nothing would save you."

"Thank you for your concern. You're probably right. I'm being stupid."

George barked in agreement.

"Yeah, you probably are, but it's an amazing feeling, isn't it?"

"It is. I feel free."

"Congratulations. A lot of people don't get to that place in their life. Do you need help turning around so you can head back down?"

"Actually, I hadn't thought of that," said Ruby, a perplexed look crossing her face.

"I didn't think you did." The girl moved gracefully to Ruby and steadied her as Ruby carefully changed position, inching her way until she was faced the opposite direction.

"Thanks. I needed that."

They both laughed, grinning at each other like maniacs.

"Well, be safe going down. If you get dizzy, crouch and hang on with both hands. There is no shame in that."

"Good advice. I think I will."

"By the way, is that your dog raising the ruckus down there?"

"Yeah, that's George."

"Well, he's worried about you, so be careful. You're very lucky to have a dog who loves you that much."

"You have no idea."

Ruby carefully made her way back down the knife-edge of the rocks. When the mountain top widened, Ruby stood up.

George stopped barking.

Ruby walked past the sign and came back to the ecstatic dog.

"Hey, buddy. I'm just fine."

George covered her face with doggy kisses. She hugged him back, pulling him close to her.

"You're a good dog. I love you, and I'm sorry I scared you. You deserve a puppy biscuit."

She sat down on the rocks next to George and rummaged in her backpack. She came up with a biscuit for him and some granola for her. She also glanced at her phone. A long list of text messages had loaded.

Most of them were from Joe. At first, he was letting her know he would be another day, because the weather hadn't been good for taking pictures. Then he started getting worried. Why hadn't he heard from her? She wasn't answering his texts. Was she okay? Then he was reassuring himself. She was fine. She was an adult. Maybe she didn't have cell reception.

Ruby smiled at that one. *Right on the nosey,* she thought.

She typed out a text letting him know she was fine and hit send. Message failed. Well, she wasn't going back up there, so he would just have to have faith. She was fine. She was more than fine. She was great.

Chapter 40

Ruby was sitting at the picnic table at her campsite, and George was curled up in the sun taking a late morning nap. Ruby was on her second cup of coffee, chewing on a pencil eraser as she edited copy on her computer. She had started writing her article about the Seneca Rocks area. She was working on a sidebar about the camping facilities. Chewing on an eraser was an old habit from college. Despite the fact that she had moved on from paper and pencil, she still needed to chew to concentrate.

She reached absently for her coffee when she heard the crunch of gravel as a vehicle pulled into the campsite next to her. Micky jumped out of his car, his arms full of grocery bags.

"Hey, Ruby. How's it going?" Micky said over his shoulder as he unlocked the old pop up.

"Good, and you? Stocking up for the week or what?" She asked, amused at the free-spirited Micky looking all domestic.

"No, I have to make a dish to share for his afternoon's reunion picnic."

"You're going to cook? On your little backpacking stove?"

Ruby hit save on her computer and ambled over to Micky's campsite. She was curious. Could climber-boy cook, too?

"I just have to boil some pasta. I'm going to make pasta salad. My ma taught me that back when I was a kid. Everyone always loved her pasta salad."

"Is your mom going to be there? Are you worried about the competition?"

Micky smiled at Ruby.

"My ma died when I was seventeen. She had breast cancer. She had no idea. When she found out, it was too late. Ma didn't like to go to doctors. She didn't trust medical tests. She always said they would just find something and make everyone crazy, cost money, then say it was nothing. She said it happened to Aunt Betty. Well, Ma wasn't lucky."

"I am so sorry, Micky."

"Thank you. At least she taught me to make good pasta salad. Hey, you want to come to an old-fashion mountain family reunion picnic? I guarantee Uncle Jose is currently roasting a hog. Everyone will bring a dish to share. We will all act pious, say prayers before we eat, and even sing a hymn or two, in four-part harmony. Then in the evening, the moonshine and fiddles will come out. Then the real party starts."

"Oh, no. I don't want to impose."

"You won't. As a matter of fact, most of these campers here belong to members of my extended family one way or another. There are probably all kinds of wild rumors about us floating around anyhow. You might as well come. If you don't, some do gooder will stop by and ask why you are being unkind to me. You don't want that to happen, do you?"

"No, I guess not. But I don't have a dish to share."

"You can help me make the pasta salad."

"Okay. I accept."

"Oh, there's just one thing."

"What's that?"

"George will need to stay here."

"Why, doesn't your family like dogs?"

"They do, but they have dogs. Big dogs. Dogs that sometimes like to fight. George wouldn't have a chance. Although the attitude he has expressed toward me might warrant him meeting my family's dogs."

George opened his napping eyes a slit and bestowed a deep threatening growl upon Micky. Micky ignored him.

George did not like being ignored.

Micky and Ruby worked side by side cleaning and cutting up vegetables. Ruby cooked the pasta in her kitchen declaring it was safer and easier than trying to cook several pounds of corkscrews on a backpacking stove. Micky looked pained that she didn't have any faith in his abilities.

Once everything was ready and the pasta rinsed in cold water, Micky mixed the ingredients in a large stainless-steel bowl and nestled it in a large cooler full of ice. Ruby looked ruefully at her t-shirt; a big oil stain from the dressing had appeared.

"Let me change into something clean and I'll be ready to go. George, go potty."

George looked pained and refused to get up.

"Seriously, George. Go potty."

Ruby disappeared into the trailer and emerged wearing a pair of denim capris and a deep green v-neck shirt. Her feet were happy in her favorite pair of flip flops.

"You didn't have to dress up for this," Micky said, looking at Ruby with a new interest.

Ruby looked at him carefully. Was he joking? How was this dressed up? He had to be pulling her leg.

She put George in the camper and gave him a couple of puppy biscuits. She reminded him to be a good dog, and she would be home later.

George was pissed.

Ruby climbed into Micky's Jeep, and he handed her the chilled bowl of pasta salad. Then he got in and started the old Wrangler. It coughed and sputtered then roared to life. Micky put it into gear and backed out of the campsite.

George howled mournfully as they drove down the campground lane away from him.

A half an hour later, Micky pulled the Jeep off the main road onto a gravel lane that seemed to head straight up. He shifted into four-wheel drive and let the Jeep pull them up the grade steadily. Ruby's heart was in her throat as they rounded a hairpin turn, the cliff on her side dropping hundreds of feet straight down. After climbing steadily, working their way up on switchbacks, Micky turned off onto an even smaller gravel lane. The Jeep growled as they descended a steep grade into a valley. Then up again. The woods opened up, and below Ruby was a beautiful vista. They had emerged onto a bald, with a small white farmhouse lit by dazzling sunshine. The house was wrapped in a wide porch with intricate gingerbread climbing on the roof supports. Two small red barns and a chicken coop flanked the house. To the side of the house, next to a small orchard were rows of tables, chairs lined up at them like a well-maintained outdoor cafeteria. Another set of long tables was set up to hold the mountains of food the guests were bringing.

Micky parked the Jeep to the side of the barn next to a long line of pickup trucks and cars in various states of repair. He helped Ruby out of the Jeep, and they made their way to the orchard. Micky walked up to the buffet table carrying the bowl he had taken from Ruby. A large woman with a gray, wispy bun relieved him of the bowl.

"Is that Molly's pasta salad?"

"Yes ma'am. I wouldn't bring any other."

"You're a good boy, Micky, despite your hair and those ridiculous earrings. Is this the young lady everyone at the campground is gossiping about."

"Yes, Aunt Mil, this is Ruby, and there is nothing to gossip about."

"Well, yes there is. They say she's pretty with stunning hair. At least they got that right. They also say you two are an item. It's obvious they got that wrong."

Ruby looked at Aunt Mil with a quizzical expression.

"Oh, don't fret, dear. It's nothing against you. You two just aren't compatible. It's not your fault. Micky is just difficult, and you are your own free spirit. Not a good match. Keep looking, Micky, dear."

Aunt Mil pecked Micky on the cheek and shook Ruby's hand.

"Make yourself at home." With that Mil flittered off, making her rounds among the guests.

"Sorry about that. Aunt Mil fancies herself as some sort of psychic. I hope that didn't bother you."

"Not in the least," Ruby replied, despite the fact that she felt unsettled.

During the next few hours, Ruby was hugged, inspected, yelled at by an old deaf uncle who felt if he couldn't hear, no one could, and adopted by a three-year-old girl who didn't speak, only smiled secretly.

She saw three dog fights and a chicken lose a couple of tail feathers to a coonhound. She also tasted her first pit roasted hog and was astounded at how tender and juicy it was. Pork had never tasted so good.

As evening closed in, true to Micky's word, the moon-shine and fiddles came out. As the drinking commenced, so did the dancing. Everyone danced, young and old, with wild abandon. Micky pulled her grinning into the circle, and after several pulls from the moonshine mason jar, Ruby set her soul free and let her feet dance to the rhythm of the mountains.

Later, in the star-studded night, Micky tucked Ruby into

the front seat of his Jeep. She smiled at him through the haze of moonshine. Aunt Mil came to say goodbye.

"You drive back carefully, Micky. Take good care of this young lady. She isn't yours to hurt. There is someone waiting for her, and he won't be happy if you bring her back damaged in any way. Do you understand me, boy?"

Micky nodded soberly. He was a little afraid of his Aunt Mil.

"Ruby, my dear, be careful to remember your heart. Your new-found freedom is precious, but too much freedom can hurt you."

Ruby just smiled and thanked Aunt Mil for a good time.

"You're welcome. You're drunk. You're a lightweight and not of mountain stock, but you are a sweet, good woman. Micky is not for you. The one who waits for you is."

"George is waiting for me," Ruby said, her eyes glassy, her lips curved in a perpetual smile.

"George is her dog," said Micky.

Aunt Mil smiled knowingly and patted Ruby's arm.

"Goodnight kids. Be careful."

Chapter 41

R uby fell asleep on the ride home, listing sideways with each turn of the switchback. Micky kept pushing her back in a sitting position. Ruby just smiled at him and closed her eyes.

Micky pulled into his campsite and was surprised to see a truck parked at Ruby's. In the dark he could make out a man sitting at the picnic table. A shadow that looked a lot like a dog was sitting next to him

"Ruby, wake up."

"Ummm. Shhh."

"Ruby. Come on. We are back at the campsite. Wake up."

"M'kay."

"Ruby, are you married?"

"Awww. That's so sweet. I'm just not ready to get married right now."

"No, I'm not asking you to marry me. I'm asking if you are already married."

"No. My husband is dead. I think he might be my dog, though. I'm so tired. Just let me sleep."

"You're not tired. You're drunk."

"No, I'm not. I'm not drunk."

"Yes, you are, and your dog is going ape shit, and there is a man sitting on your picnic table with him."

"Nope. Not drunk."

"Shit," cursed Micky, under his breath. "This is about to get messy. Damn Aunt Mil."

Micky climbed out of the Jeep, glancing over at Ruby. She was leaning against her door, snoring slightly with a slight smile on her face and a bit of drool gathered at the corner of her mouth.

He walked over to Ruby's campsite.

George moved to attack.

"George, stay," Joe commanded.

Why? the dog growled. *Just let me bite him a little.*

Joe smiled grimly and stood up, resisting the urge to brush off the seat of his pants.

"Evenin'," Micky said, reaching out his right hand. "I'm Micky."

"Where's Ruby?" Joe asked not returning the handshake.

Nice, George stood, growling.

"Ruby is in the front seat of my Jeep. She's sleeping."

Joe brushed past Micky, walking purposefully to the passenger side of the Jeep.

George took it as a sign and leapt for Micky.

"George, no," Joe tossed over his shoulder.

George stopped mid-air and landed on all fours. Micky just stared at the dog, not giving ground.

"Dog, back off. Ruby is fine," Micky drawled, unconcerned.

Joe opened the door of the Jeep and caught Ruby as she slid sideways, falling out of the vehicle.

"Good Lord, you're drunk," said Joe.

"Hey, Joe. Where you been?" Ruby smiled sweetly.

"Working, and you?"

"I've been dancing. With people who have long beards and play fiddles and who drink from Mason jars."

"Really?"

"I was doing research."

"Research?"

"Yes. Did you ever drink moonshine? I like mojitos better, but I think I can dance better when I drink moonshine."

"I think you'll change your mind about moonshine in the morning, honey. Come on."

Joe lifted Ruby out of the Jeep and carried her to her camper. George jumped up and ran to them. He reared up on his hind legs to give Ruby a sniff and reassure himself of her safety.

He sneezed.

What the hell? George sneeze again. *She stinks.*

"Hop down, George. She's been partying a bit too hard."

Micky reached out and opened Ruby's camper door so Joe could pass through with the now sleeping Ruby.

"You stay here," Joe growled at Micky.

George growled, too. He approved.

Micky sat down at the picnic table to wait.

Fifteen minutes later, Joe and George emerged from the camper. George sneezing steadily.

"I might suggest you put a garbage can or bucket by the bed," Micky drawled with a smile

"Already done. Made sure it was lined with a garbage bag and left a roll of paper towels next to it, too."

"This ain't your first rodeo."

"Not by a long shot. Okay, let's try this again. I'm Joe. I'm Ruby's friend. Good friend."

George moved next to Joe and sat leaning against him. Affirming his place in their lives.

"Like I said before. I'm Micky. I'm Ruby's new friend. Friend without benefits, in case you were worried."

"Friend who gets her drunk?"

"Friend who didn't realize she was a lightweight."

"Friend who should have thought about the fact that most Northerners haven't consumed much in the way of moonshine.'

"Point taken."

"Can I ask why she was drinking all this moonshine?"

"Well, this campground is filled with relatives of mine, some several times removed, because they are in town for our annual family reunion. I invited Ruby to come. She said yes. The family is very happy to share their food, and they expect you to partake of their moonshine."

"Didn't you think she had had enough?"

"Truthfully, she spent so much time dancing with Junior that I didn't see her much once those fiddles started playing. Junior probably was the one to give her most of the moonshine."

"What else did this Junior guy do?" Joe was starting to get annoyed all over again.

George looked at Joe and agreed. He was annoyed, too.

"Well, I do know that Junior does enjoy dancing with pretty ladies. Sometimes, he tries to sneak off with them to the barn and take them up to the hayloft." Micky looked sideways at Joe, enjoying the reaction.

"Did he take Ruby to the hayloft?" ask Joe, his jaw tense.

"Nah. He got a leg cramp, and Aunt Ada brought him his walker and made him sit down. The whole time she was reminding him that he was eighty-two years old and needed to mind his heart." Micky smiled at Joe, and Joe laughed unexpectedly.

"So, it's my turn to ask some questions, if you don't mind." Micky looked steadily at Joe. "You said you were a good friend. Ruby didn't mention you specifically, but she did say a friend was going to join her. She was worried about her friend finding a camping spot. I assume the friend is you?"

"Yes, you can assume that."

"She also kept checking for messages, but I'm sure you've noticed that there isn't any cell service here."

"Yes, I've noticed that. I figured that she was having trouble reaching me. I wasn't worried until I got here and found George in the camper and her Jeep here."

"If it would have been me, I would have been pretty concerned."

"I was at first, but George was sad, not scared."

"I think you're putting too much stock in a dog."

"Trust me, I'm not. By the way, he doesn't like you."

"Ruby says he doesn't like anyone."

"You'll notice he likes me."

Lesser of two evils, George sneezed again.

Joe reached over and scratched George's ears. George stretched his neck upward, his eyes closed in slits, enjoying the attention.

"Yes. I assume Ruby likes you, too."

"Yes, she does."

"Okay. Did you find a campsite?"

"I did. On the other side of the campgrounds."

"I'm glad you found a place. Well, I'm going to say goodnight. It was a pleasure to meet you, Joe. Good night."

Micky shook Joe's hand, ignored George, and walked over to his own camper, whistling softly as he walked. In minutes he was in his pop-up and the lights were out.

I don't like him. Not at all. George stretched and walked to the camper and barked softly.

"He's not so bad. He's just a kid."

Don't underestimate him. George woofed again. *She liked his muscles.*

Joe unconsciously flexed as he got up and let the dog into the camper. He followed locking the door behind him and turning out the lights.

Chapter 42

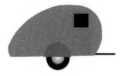

The sound of retching woke Joe from a sound sleep. He opened his eyes to see Ruby's beautiful hair hanging on all sides of the wastebasket as she vomited repeatedly.

"Morning, baby," Joe greeted her enthusiastically

Ruby groaned.

George whined and wrinkled his nose. He looked up at Joe, woofed and ran for the door.

"Excuse me, sweetheart. George needs to go out."

Ruby groaned again.

"Would you like me to let him out for you?" Joe asked sweetly.

"Asshole," Ruby managed to murmur between bouts of vomiting.

Joe let the dog out, tying him to the chain hooked to the awning. George snarled at Joe.

"Sorry, buddy. I can only take care of one of you at a time."

Ruby was right, George looked back at Joe as he moved away from the trailer.

Love you, too, George. Love you, too.

Back inside the trailer, Joe rummaged through Ruby's things in the bathroom, coming up with a pony tail band.

He walked back to Ruby and placed a cool, wet facecloth on the back of her neck, then pulled her hair back from around the bucket and fastened in into a ponytail.

"Thanks," Ruby gasped.

He stepped to the kitchen and got another garbage bag. Swiftly he replaced the bag, tying the full one quickly. He moved it outside the trailer so he could take it to the dumpster later.

Micky saluted Joe with a cup of coffee as he sat contemplating the rock face of the mountain before him.

"Morning," said Joe cheerfully.

"Morning. Coffee?"

"Sure, thanks."

Joe popped his head in the camper and checked Ruby. She was curled on the bed, her head hanging over. She was panting but alive.

Micky had disappeared into his popup and reemerged with a steaming cup of coffee.

"I figured it wouldn't hurt to have a pot ready."

"I've changed my mind about you. You're a good man."

"Don't say that until you've tasted my coffee." Micky grinned.

Joe carefully sipped the black brew. It was strong. It was smooth. It was delicious.

"Damn good cup of coffee. Thank you."

"No worries. I'm afraid you have a long morning ahead of you."

"I think Ruby has a longer morning ahead of her." Joe walked back to the trailer and peeked in at Ruby. She was asleep. Micky followed, and the two of them sat at the picnic table enjoying their coffee in silence.

Micky picked up the empty cups and went back to his popup. Joe waved a thanks and went back inside to check Ruby. She was soundly sleeping. He filled a glass with water and sat it next to the wastebasket. Then he kissed Ruby on the forehead.

"I'm taking George for a walk. I'll be back."

"M'kay."

"There is a glass of water on the floor for you if you need it."

"Mmmm."

He kissed her again and pulled the covers over her shoulders. She snuggled down into the sheets and began to snore softly.

"Would you like to go for a walk, George?" Joe asked, as he pulled the camper door closed behind him.

George jumped down from the camp chair and sat in front of Joe, waiting for him to snap the lead onto his collar.

They started down the campground road when Micky came out of his popup shrugging on his climbing backpack.

"Where ya headin'?" he asked as he straightened the shoulder strap.

"I figured Ruby is going to sleep it off, so I decided George needed some exercise."

"I'm heading over to do some climbing. There's a nice trail up to the top of Seneca Rocks if you want to have a nice hike. Ruby did it the other day. I would get some water to take along. It's going to be warm again today."

"Sounds like a plan." Joe stopped at his truck and picked up his backpack and some waters. Then he and Micky walked together companionably toward the mountain, an anxious George trotting between them. He looked back at the trailer and whined.

"She'll be okay, buddy. No worries. Ruby just needs some rest."

Chapter 43

Three hours later Joe and George came back to the camper. Micky's campsite was vacated of the popup, and the camp host was putting a reserved paper on the post for the next camper.

Joe knocked softly before he opened the door. The bed was empty, the sheets stripped. The wastebasket was no longer next to the bed. He could hear the shower running, and George sniffed at the bathroom door, wagging his tail.

Joe knocked softly at the door.

"Ruby, I'm back. Are you okay?"

"I'll be out in a minute."

"I have some chicken soup. Would you like me to warm it up?"

"You and your chicken soup. Sure. I think that sounds good, but I'm guessing it's not Laura's."

"True, but beggars can't be choosers."

Joe pulled a pan out of the small cupboard and opened the cans of soup he bought at the small camper store down the road. He put the pan on the small propane stove and began heating the soup.

Ruby emerged from the bathroom wrapped in a towel and running the comb through her long auburn hair.

"Here, let me do that for you." Joe took the comb and pulled it gently through her hair.

George growled half-heartedly.

"Are you feeling better?" Joe asked as he nuzzled her neck, drawing her damp body close to his.

"Yeah. I have a headache, and my stomach is still a little queasy, but the soup smells good."

"It's probably ready. What would you like to drink? Mojito?" Joe teased.

Ruby laughed.

"No, I think water will be just fine."

Joe carried the soup bowls outside to the picnic table. Ruby slipped her shirt and shorts on, then slid her feet into her flip flops. She brought out two soup spoons and two glasses of water.

George followed carrying a large rawhide.

"Where'd he get that?" Ruby asked.

"They had them at the camp store. I just thought George deserved one."

"It's probably not good for him, but, oh, what the hell."

George wagged his tail and settled on the ground near his camp chair. He turned his head sideways gnawing on the bone held vertically in his paws.

At that moment, George's suspicions were confirmed. Joe was a whole lot better than Micky.

When they were done, Ruby's color had returned, and she was starting to look like herself.

"I need to wash those sheets."

"So, we need to find a laundry?"

"I'm afraid so. That's the one thing I absolutely hate about traveling like this. I hate laundromats. I got spoiled at Laura and Ben's."

"I hate them, too. Maybe it won't be so bad when we do it together. Gather your stuff and we will find a place. My guess is we'll have to drive into Elkins to find a place, but I don't mind. Are you up to it?"

"I think so."

With that Ruby went inside to pick up the sheets. Then she came out of the camper and pulled a small duffel bag out of her Jeep. She held it up to show Joe.

"Dirty laundry, detergent and softener. By the way, I never asked. Where's your camper?"

"On the other side of the campground. Get in the truck, and we'll get my laundry and go. George will probably need a nap. We hiked up to the top of Seneca Rocks today."

"Ha, that's twice for him. Did he go out on the platform with you?"

"No, he refused."

"Figures."

They put George in the camper, and Ruby grabbed her hotspot and laptop. George lay down on his pillow and watched as Joe and Ruby closed and locked the door. Joe helped Ruby into the truck, then he got in the other side. Putting the truck in reverse, Joe glanced over at Ruby.

"Was your husband afraid of heights?"

"Yep."

"Figures."

Chapter 44

They wound through the mountains heading down into the small college town of Elkins. They found a laundromat near the college that was relatively empty. While the laundry was washing, Ruby worked on her newest editing assignment from Laney, "Helping your Honey Check His Jewels; A Step by Step Guide for Examining for Testicular Cancer", and Joe worked on his latest hotel shoot, photoshopping the images to perfection. They worked companionably side by side, occasionally reaching out and touching each other absently. When their laundry was dry, they folded it together, arguing about the proper way to fold a towel.

"Are you hungry?" Joe asked Ruby as they finished folding her sheets.

"You heard my stomach growling." Ruby said, blushing.

"I did, but I wasn't sure if it was upset still or if you were ready to eat a full meal."

"No, I'm ready for a full meal. More than ready, actually. I might be starving."

"You were really drunk, but you recovered fast. I'm impressed."

"Don't be. After you left, I woke up and threw up a million more times. I saw you and George were gone, and I was jealous and felt sorry for myself. Then I puked again and fell asleep. I woke up later with puke in my hair. It wasn't pretty."

"I think I might be glad I was gone so long."

"I know I'm glad you were gone so long. So embarrassing!"

Joe pulled her to him and kissed the top of her head.

"A hangover isn't catching," Ruby teased, "and I brushed my teeth a couple of times."

Joe grinned and tipped her face up to his. They were alone in the brightly lit laundromat. He bent and kissed her deeply. She dropped the towel they had just folded onto the bench and melted into his chest. Joe's arms came around her protectively, wrapping her in his warmth. When they finally pulled away from each other, they realized a young couple was waiting patiently for them to move so they could get past them to an empty set of machines.

Ruby shyly mumbled her apologies, while Joe gathered the laundry in their duffel bags. He was grinning. The other couples were grinning. Ruby was embarrassed.

Just as they were going out the door, Joe turned and asked the couple where they could get something to eat in a nice quiet setting.

The couple enthusiastically shared their favorite dining spots and wished them a good evening, smiling indulgently at Ruby and Joe.

"Damn," said Ruby as they loaded the laundry in the truck.

"What?"

"I feel like those kids in there thought we were cute cause we were like grandparents or something kissing in public. I'm not that old!" Ruby protested.

"Not old, not you. Mature maybe, in a sexy sort of way."

Joe ducked as Ruby smacked him on the shoulder with a box of softener sheets.

"With maturity comes experience," she threatened.

"That sounds promising."

"Yeah, well, I'm hungry and feeling insulted. You have some groveling to do."

Ruby smiled happily as they loaded the clean laundry into the truck. She had missed Joe more than she realized, and she was very happy he was back. Very happy.

Ruby and Joe drove past the dining spots recommended by the young couple. The venues were busy and bright, full of young people enjoying the evening. Each time, Ruby and Joe looked at each other and shook their heads. Not interested.

"I'm sure one of those places would be fine," said Ruby, feeling a little irritated.

Joe raised an eyebrow at her. She was staring straight ahead out the front window.

"Uh oh. You are seriously hungry, aren't you?"

Ruby started to retort and caught herself.

"Yeah, I guess I am. Sometimes when I get really hungry, I get a little cranky."

"I was guessing that. I've got this." Joe pulled the truck into a minimart parking lot and pulled out his phone. Ruby tried her best to let him.

A few minutes later he put the truck in drive and headed confidently down the street.

"Where are we going?" Ruby asked.

"I think I found a place that will work."

"Where?"

"Up the road a bit."

"How far?"

"Not too…"

"You're going to be impossible, aren't you?"

"Probably."

Ruby crossed her arms across her chest and slumped down in the seat. She knew she was being petty, but she wasn't used to not making the decisions. Even when she was married to George, she was the one who decided where to go and what to do. George just liked to go along for the ride.

This was a power play, and Ruby knew it. The question was how to play it on her end. She didn't want to be a bitch, but she was feeling the irritation crawling up her spine.

Joe looked over at her and smiled sweetly. She smiled back, trying hard to look nonchalant.

Joe burst out laughing. She wasn't fooling anyone.

That pissed her off even more.

Damn, he was winning.

"Um," she said, her voice dripping with sugar," we just left the city limits and are heading back into the mountains. You are aware of that, right?"

"Yes, ma'am."

"There wasn't anything on the way here. We didn't pass anything that looked remotely like a restaurant."

"I know," he said, equally as saccharin.

Ruby sighed, a little too loudly.

"What? You don't have any faith in me?" he asked.

"I do. Okay. I'll just sit here."

"Wasn't that what you have been doing?"

Damn, he got her, and by the look on his face, he knew it.

The truck slowed, and Joe turned on a small road that led back into a tunnel of trees. On the right side of the road, a mountain stream rushed by.

"Where?"

"Shhh…" he told her.

As the truck rounded a corner, lights twinkled between some trees ahead. As they drew closer, a log lodge came into view, situated on the side of the rushing stream. A second story deck wrapped around the structure with dining tables set under tiny intimate lights, creating a private feel for each area.

Ruby exhaled.

"This is beautiful. This is perfect."

Joe just grinned at her and tapped his phone.

"You can thank technology for tonight's dining experience."

They were welcomed graciously by the hostess and seated at a table on the balcony at the corner. They were cantilevered over the stream and the effect was delightful.

"Wine?" Joe asked her, "Or are you gun shy?"

"No. I would love some."

Joe showed the waitress his selection and she smiled her approval. She told them the specials for the evening then left to get their wine.

"Joe this is perfect. I'm sorry I was cranky earlier."

"Honey, if that is as cranky as you get, we're good!" He leaned over the table and stroked her cheek, running his fingers lightly under her jaw. "I'll take this cranky anytime."

The waitress returned with the wine and a loaf of warm Italian bread, butter drizzling off the top of the loaf.

Ruby nearly swooned.

They both selected the pan-seared rainbow trout and then settled back to enjoy the wine and bread until their entrees came.

Ruby felt the tension she felt earlier slip away as she nibbled on the buttery, salty bread.

"Good?" asked Joe.

"Delicious."

"I missed you, Ruby. A lot."

"I know. I missed you, too."

"Well, I think you filled your time with a little more fun than I managed to," Joe said ruefully.

Ruby blushed, furiously.

"I'm sorry about that whole hungover thing. That has

never happened to me before. You know there was nothing between Micky and me, right?"

"Yes, I know that, but you aren't committed to me. I don't own you, and you have a right to make your own decisions," said Joe, trying to sound completely convincing.

"You're right. I do have that right. I'm glad you recognize that. I like you very much. You have become important to me. I just don't know how important or…" her voice trailed off.

"You don't have to know, and I'm not trying to pressure you. I just wanted you to know that I was worried about you, and admittedly jealous when I saw you in that Jeep with that kid."

"Kid?" Ruby laughed. "He's not a kid. Although, he certainly has a young, well-muscled body," she teased wickedly.

Joe swallowed hard and gulped his wine.

"Joe, I had a great time at the reunion. I met some wonderful people who showed me what life in the mountains is like. Micky is a nice guy, but not my type. I will admit, I enjoy the fact that you're jealous of that whole thing. That's a new experience for me."

"Don't use that too often," Joe growled.

"You sound like George, getting all feisty."

They were rescued by the waitress who placed steaming plates of trout with jasmine rice in front of them. They both looked at each other and smiled, then dug in.

An hour later, as Ruby polished off a slice of chocolate cake covered in ganache, she leaned back in her chair and closed her eyes. A light breeze lifted her hair, and the sound of the stream soothed her.

"You are so beautiful. You know that, right?"

She opened her eyes to see Joe staring at her, a new hunger in his eyes. She ducked her head looking up through her lashes.

"Thank you," she whispered.

"Let's get out of here, " he said in a husky voice.

Joe paid the bill, leaving a generous tip. He took Ruby by the hand and led her to his truck, his index finger tracing circles in her palm causing her stomach to flip in anticipation.

Chapter 45

J oe pulled out of the parking lot and turned the truck toward the campground. He played with Ruby's hair as they drove in silence. Suddenly, he put his blinker on and took a right onto a forest service road. The truck bounced along in the darkness, the headlights making crazy shadows in the trees.

"Where?" Ruby started to ask.

"Shhh," Joe told her, touching his finger to his lips.

He turned at a sign that announced a picnic area and scenic overlook.

"I don't think we're going to be able to see anything very scenic, and I am too full for a picnic," Ruby said lightly.

"I'm still hungry, " Joe warned.

He parked his truck and reached into the back seat. He pulled his woven beach blanket out and got out of the truck. Ruby waited until he opened her door for her. She was beginning to like the direction Joe's thoughts were heading.

He led her to the overlook and then found a path that wound down through the trees. As their eyes adjusted to the darkness, Ruby discovered that she could see quite well. Joe pulled her out onto a flat rock that over looked the valley below. In the darkness, Ruby could see lights twinkling, a testament to the civilization that gathered in the valley. The side of the mountain was shrouded in darkness.

Joe spread the blanket onto the moss covered stone and pulled Ruby on top of him. He nuzzled her neck, rejoicing in her glorious mane that cascaded over his head, circling them in an intimate space.

Ruby kissed him, and he responded with hunger. His arms wrapped around her waist, and his right hand moved up the inside of her shirt, tracing the indention of her backbone. In a deft moment, he unhooked her bra, freeing her breast that hung above him.

Ruby moaned and ground her hips into Joe, urging him to continue what he started.

He obliged, unbuttoning her shirt, freeing her body to the moonlight. They made love on the edge of the cliff as the night sounds stilled to listen to their song.

"Why doesn't the rock hurt my knees while we're making love, but when we're done, it's a different story altogether," Ruby moaned as she rolled off Joe. He caught her and eased her gently on her back. The rock was a lot more comfortable in that position.

They lay side by side, their heads touching, holding hands, gazing at the stars above them. The moon was low on the horizon, and the stars were dazzling, pressing down on them, a universe still to be explored.

"It's crazy, but I feel like there are more stars here than at home," Ruby said, awestruck at the sheer volume of the twinkling lights.

"That's because you're closer to them, you know, altitude," Joe said matter-of-factly.

"You're kidding, right?" Ruby looked at him to see if he really believed that.

Joe busted out laughing.

"I love you, Ruby."

Everything stopped.

Breathing stopped.

The night sounds stopped.

Everything was waiting.

"I'm sorry, Ruby. I didn't mean to do that." Joe scrubbed his face with his hands, frustrated with himself.

Ruby held stock still. She didn't know what to think. What to feel. She didn't know.

Chapter 46

The drive back to the campground was quiet. Joe tried to apologize another time, but Ruby waved him off. Told him not to worry about it.

It was obvious he needed to worry about it.

Joe stopped the truck in front of Ruby's teardrop and got out of the truck.

"It's okay, Joe. I'm tired. I had a lovely evening. Really, I did, but I'm tired…"

"I was just going to help you carry your laundry in," he replied quietly.

Ruby knew there was no point arguing with him. He was going to carry that laundry bag. She unlocked the camper door and let an awaiting George out to do his business. George greeted Ruby like she had been gone for days, then glanced up at Joe before he trotted out to the bushes.

What the heck? George stared at Joe from under a bush.

Let it go.

That's not even fun. George sneezed.

Not tonight, buddy.

George finished and ran up to Joe, demanding a scratch behind the ears. *Something's really wrong. Is Ruby okay? DID YOU HURT HER?* George bared his teeth at Joe.

"Joe, I'm really tired. I'd like to go to bed."

"Goodnight, Ruby. I'm sorry. I didn't mean to…"

"I know, Joe." Ruby turned to close the door, George scooting in at the last minute.

I really screwed up, buddy. You win.

As Joe turned to leave, he heard the sound of crying from the camper. He couldn't tell if it was Ruby or the damned dog.

Joe pulled up to his own camper. He opened the door and put the laundry duffel on his bed. His camper was a lot smaller than Ruby's. The inside of his was only a bed with a side table that flipped up from the door. He crawled in next to the duffel and spent the next few minutes putting his clothes in his cabinets. He was frustrated and angry with himself. He knew Ruby wasn't ready. He wasn't either. He didn't even know that was going to come out of his mouth. It just happened. It was just right.

But it wasn't. Not for her. Not for Ruby.

He went back outside and sat in his camp chair. Sleep wasn't going to come tonight. He started a small fire and settled in to stare at it. His mind wouldn't rest. He didn't know what he was going to do. How was he going to mend the damage he caused?

Ruby sat up from her bed where she had thrown herself after she closed the door on Joe. George had curled up against her, his muzzle tucked under her chin. He lay quietly, letting her cry out her pain. He didn't know what to do. He didn't know how to help her.

When she sat up, George sat up, too and looked at her expectantly. She reached out and gathered him into her arms.

"Oh George, what am I going to do? I blew it. I was a total bitch."

George reached up and licked her chin, trying to make her feel better. He was bewildered. He missed something and was trying hard to figure everything out.

"When he told me he loved me, I froze."

Uh oh. Well, that explains it. Smooth move, cowboy.

No shit.

George was startled. Joe was back at his camper, wasn't he? George listened and sniffed. Did Joe come back? George sniffed again. No, Joe wasn't here.

Ruby put the tea kettle on and stared into space as she waited for the water to boil. She was tired but wide awake, her eyes swollen from crying.

"What a stupid roller coaster ride these last couple of days have been, George." The dog cocked his head, his ears perking up, listening to her. His lady was sad.

The tea kettle whistled merrily, making Ruby feel even sadder. As she made herself some chamomile tea, she thought about how she reacted to Joe's declaration.

"I was rude," Ruby announced to George. "I was rude, and not thoughtful. I was only thinking of myself and not Joe. I can't imagine how he is feeling."

Sipping on the tea and leaning against the counter, she was feeling herself getting even more aggravated. The chamomile tea should be calming, not making her even more wound up.

She wrapped both hands around the mug, drawing up the heat into her soul, allowing herself to be wrapped in the hug of warmth, but it didn't work. She didn't feel hugged. She felt alone.

George whined.

"What's wrong, George?"

He ran to the door and whined again.

"You have to go outside?"

Woof.

"You know. That's a good idea. You want to go for a walk? Maybe that'll settle me down. What do you say?"

George danced around in a circle, urging Ruby to get a move on. Ruby slipped her feet into her shoes and grabbed her zip-up hoody. She snapped on George's leash and stepped out into the night.

It was late. The moon was high overhead, making it easy to see. She and George cast moon shadows on the side of the camp road as they walked. Usually Ruby loved to look at moon shadows, thinking they were some of the coolest things ever, but tonight they meant nothing to her.

She tried to make her mind blank as she walked. The campground was quiet, even the late night crowd had turned in. Ruby listened to the sounds of her shoes crunching on the gravel of the camp road. It seemed incredibly loud in the silence of the mountains.

George started pulling on his leash and looking back at Ruby as if to tell her to hurry up. She picked up the pace a little.

"Sorry buddy. I'm not paying attention." She curved around and turned onto another camp road passing RV's and tents tucked in among the trees.

George trotted happily in front of Ruby, leading the way, his tail held high. Ruby breathed deeply trying to clear her mind. She caught the whiff of a campfire. Within minutes she caught sight of a small fire still burning merrily in the night.

"Idiots," she said to George. "This is how forest fires start."

Then she saw the lone figure of a man sitting at the fire. Suddenly, she realized she was looking at the backside of Joe's campsite.

George pulled eagerly on his leash, his tail wagging.

Ruby stopped in the road.

Indecisive.

George made the decision for her.

Woof.

Joe turned and peered into the darkness. Ruby realized that the light from the fire was blinding Joe, and he probably couldn't see her.

"Ruby?" Joe's voice softly questioned.

She slipped between the trees and skirted around a sleeping popup trailer. She stopped at the edge of Joe's fire ring.

George sat quietly, just the tip of his tail wagging.

George was tense.

"Hey," Ruby said feeling extremely awkward.

"Hey, yourself," Joe replied.

"Is it okay if I join you, or would you rather be alone?"

"Do you want the truth?"

"I don't know."

"Okay. Well, let's put it this way. You're welcome to have a seat and share my campfire. How's that?"

"That'll work."

Joe stood up, offering Ruby his chair. He pulled his spare out of the back of the truck.

"Sorry, George. That's all I have."

George growled at Joe for effect, then sat up in front of Ruby. She patted her lap and George jumped up, laying down so that his chin rested on her arm.

They sat quietly staring into the flames, each one lost in their own thoughts.

"I'm sorry, Joe."

"For what?"

"For acting like a little bitch, for one."

Joe snorted and sighed.

"You weren't a little bitch. I threw you a curve ball, and you didn't know how to respond. At least you didn't lie to me and tell me you love me, too." Joe said, a trace of bitterness touching his voice.

Easy, cowboy. George snapped at a bug.

"I've no intentions of ever lying to you. I only want to be honest. I'm confused. I'm scared, and I'm sad," Ruby admitted.

"Yeah, that about sums it up on my end, too."

Are you trying to make her mad? Seriously, you've never seen her mad! George started to nervously bite his right paw, digging with his nose and making snorting sounds.

"George, stop that."

Ruby nervously scratched the dog's ears, not sure what to say next.

"I couldn't sleep. I even made chamomile tea and couldn't sleep."

"I could try to find you some moonshine."

Oh, shit. George placed a paw over his nose.

Ruby tensed, about to give a sharp retort when she realized that she could see Joe's white teeth in the firelight, and he was smiling.

"Do you have any?" Ruby asked sweetly.

"Fresh out. If I had some, I probably wouldn't be sitting upright at this point."

"Joe, I really am sorry. I care about you. Deeply. I'm just not ready for the next step, or any step for that matter."

"Ruby, I know. I'm not ready, either. Honestly, it just came out of my mouth. I didn't plan it. I didn't know it was coming. It just did. I don't regret saying it because I obviously meant it, but I regret scaring you. I regret the timing. Does that make sense? Can you forgive me for scaring you?"

"Joe, there's nothing to forgive. I just hope you can forgive me for my childish reaction."

"There's nothing to forgive."

Chapter 47

R uby woke up to her alarm beeping insistently. She reached to hit snooze for the third time when she sat bolt upright. She looked over at the clock in a panic. She had one hour until her interview with the climbing instructor.

"Shit," she said out loud.

George opened one eye and looked at her, unamused. He didn't know what the panic was all about. All he knew was he didn't get to bed until three in the morning, and now he needed some sleep. He growled and burrowed deeper into the blankets, his nose pressed hard into the pillow. He squeezed his eyes shut tightly. Maybe Ruby would get the message and stop running around like a maniac.

"Come on, George. Let's go outside and go potty."

George pretended not to hear. She could go outside and go potty all by herself.

"George, let's go. I'm in a hurry."

George recognized the exasperation in his Ruby's voice. It would go better for him if he would just run outside and quickly hike a leg. The faster he did that, the faster he could crawl back in bed.

He groaned as he stood up and stretched luxuriously. Ruby was tapping her foot impatiently. He had half a mind to push her over the edge. After all, it would be easy to do after last night's drama. She was impossible. Joe was cranky, and it annoyed George. He wasn't sure why. He had liked it before when they were at odds, but this was different. This felt serious, and he wasn't sure how he felt about that. When he walked back to the camper with Ruby, she was calmer. Ruby and Joe had kissed goodnight, but it wasn't the kind of kiss that made George crazy. It was chaste. The air didn't snap with electricity like it had before. George really didn't know how he felt about that.

"Are you quite finished stretching? Get outside. Please!"

George smiled at Ruby and wagged his tail. He obediently hopped off the bed and flew out of the trailer. He peed on the first bush available and ran back in the camper, jumping on the bed and laying on the pillow. He didn't even sit up for his potty puppy biscuit. Besides, he knew she would throw it to him anyhow and bitch about the crumbs on the pillow.

"Here's your biscuit. Come get it." She waited for him to jump down. "Oh, for heaven's sake." She tossed the biscuit on the bed. "I'm going to have crumbs on my pillow tonight. I just know it."

With that, Ruby grabbed her backpack with her notebook, laptop, pens, and camera.

"Be good, George. I'll be back in a little bit."

She stepped out of the camper and locked up. She had a short hike down to the climbing shop at the base of the side road. If she hurried, she would just make it.

As she hiked past Joe's camper, she couldn't help but turn at look at his campsite. His truck was gone. He was up and already out and about. He had mentioned getting some pictures of the trout stream and the restaurant they ate at last night. He was going to drop his card and drum up some business. He told her he would catch up with her later. He wasn't pushy, and she was non-committal.

They both needed some time to think.

She walked into the climbing shop with one minute to spare. The climbing instructor was waiting for her. An hour later, she had enough information to write a nice article and wrap up her stay here.

She emailed her editor and let her know that she should have the article for the magazine by the end of the day. Ruby also let her editor know that her queue was cleaned out and she needed some more articles to work on. When Ruby hit send, she realized that it was futile. She still didn't have any service.

She hiked back up to her camper, noticing Joe still wasn't back, and woke George up again.

"Hey buddy, want to go for a ride in the Jeep? We can go find a place to eat, and I can find some Wi-Fi. What do you say?"

George sailed out of the camper in a big leap, hitting the ground with a happy grin. He ran to the Jeep and barked a hurry-up-let-me-in bark.

R uby pulled into Elkins and found a little sandwich shop near the college. She was tired, feeling the effects of last night's late night, and she could use a hot sandwich and a strong cup of coffee. There was no parking in front of the building, so she drove around until she found a space on a side street.

"Come on, buddy. Let's see if the shop owner is dog friend-ly." George waited patiently while Ruby attached his leash. Then he jumped out of the Jeep and started trotting smartly down the street. He liked hanging with his Ruby, and he wanted her to be happy and carefree, too. She really didn't feel that way now. He could tell.

Ruby knocked on the sandwich shop door, poking her head in.

"Hello? Excuse me, but do you allow dogs?"

A girl with purple hair and a blue bandanna popped her head above the counter where she had been crouching.

"Sure, as long as he's polite and isn't full of fleas."

George peeked around Ruby and gave the girl a pained look. He walked in with as much dignity as he could muster.

"No, he's clean and well-mannered. Thank you."

"No problem. What can I get you?"

"I'd love a cup of coffee, and a corned beef and swiss sandwich. I am also hoping I can get cell service here. I need to check my emails."

"Coming right up, and you should have no problem with service. Let me guess, you were up in the mountains."

"Yeah, at the campgrounds near Seneca Rocks."

"No service there, that's for sure. By the way, my name is Leigh." Leigh reached over the counter and handed Ruby her cup of coffee.

"Hi, Leigh. I'm Ruby."

"Nice to meet you, Ruby. I'll have that sandwich for you in just a minute. Mustard?"

"No, thanks."

Ruby sat at a small table in the corner and sipped on her coffee. It was strong and delicious. Joe would love this. She shook her head and opened her laptop. Her email started to go crazy, downloading a bunch of messages from her editor.

Leigh quietly put the sandwich and a side of chips on the table next to Ruby's laptop and slipped away allowing Ruby her privacy. George smiled at Leigh, so she tossed him a potato chip.

George was in love.

Ruby made sure the email was sent to her editor and then she worked her way through the emails. She found several new assignments awaiting her. Normally she found joy in new assignments, especially ones with intriguing titles like "Jocks and Socks; Fuzzy Finds for Your Favorite Fling", but she didn't even smile at that one.

George looked up at her from under the table and whined softly.

Ruby pulled out her notes, took a bite from the sandwich and got to work on her climbing article.

The sandwich was good and the coffee restorative. She was well into the article when the bell over the door to the shop tinkled. She didn't pay attention to it, not looking up from her work.

George looked.

George wagged his tail.

George was happy to see the man who walked into the sandwich shop.

Well, look what the cat dragged in. George yawned. *Good timing.*

They'll let just about anyone in here, won't they? Joe grinned at the dog.

"Hello. What can I get you?"

"I'll have what she's having," said Joe.

Ruby still didn't look up.

"Corned beef and swiss with no mustard?"

"Yes, please, but add the mustard. Some people have no taste whatsoever."

Leigh grinned.

"Coffee, too?"

"Absolutely."

Joe waited patiently, leaning against the counter watching the top of Ruby's bent head as she chewed on her pencil, thinking then typing. Thinking then typing.

Leigh put the coffee up on the counter and worked on the sandwich. Joe stayed where he was, still watching Ruby.

George watched Joe.

Joe's heart swelled. He loved this woman. He said it last night because it was so true. He just had to be careful not to lose her.

Yeah, no shit. George sneezed.

Ruby looked up.

And froze.

"Fancy meeting you here," Joe said easily as he walked over to her.

"Hello. How did you know I was here?"

"I didn't. I was hungry, and I spotted this place. I was taking pictures across the street on the campus."

"Did you get some good shots?"

"I think so. I got some great shots of the restaurant we ate at last night, and the owner bought some. He wants to use them on his website. I also convinced him he needs a brochure. Where's your Jeep?"

"I parked it down some side street. There wasn't any parking out front."

Leigh brought Joe's sandwich over to the table smiling at him. A little too flirty for Ruby's liking.

"Will you be joining her, or should I set this on a different table?"

Joe raise his eyebrows at Ruby.

She smiled warmly at him, claiming him in front of the interested Leigh.

"He'll be joining me. We're together."

Under the table, George thumped his tail against the floor in an ecstatic wag.

Chapter 48

Joe walked Ruby to her Jeep slipping George a couple of potato chips as he helped the dog into the front seat. George reminded himself that this Joe guy was really okay.

"So, what are you doing for the rest of the day?" asked Joe.

"I don't know. I'm kind of tired. I had a late night last night."

"Oh yeah? Anyone I know?"

"No. Some guy. You wouldn't know him. He was kind of cranky. Not like you. You're always smiling," Ruby teased.

"I try."

"Do you want to share dinner tonight? We could do some campfire cooking. Your trailer or mine." Ruby said hopefully.

"That sounds great. I'll bring the steaks."

"Okay, and I'll bring something I find at the grocery store, once I find one of those."

"I need to find one of those, too. Why don't you stay here, and I'll get the truck. Then you follow me, and we'll find somewhere to buy our feast. Deal?" asked Joe, his eyes sparkling.

"Deal!" said Ruby, finally feeling like her world was right again.

Deal, barked George.

R uby followed Joe into a medium-sized supermarket on the edge of town. She rolled down the windows partway and put some water in a dish for George. Satisfied he was going to be okay waiting in the Jeep, she got out and locked up. Joe was waiting for her.

Absently, he reached out his hand, catching hers in his. She smiled when he looked embarrassed and started to apologize.

"Stop. Look, we still like each other, right? We probably have to talk more about the other night, figure out where we're going, but I think we're okay, right? I mean, I'm okay with you holding my hand, and I think you're okay with this, right?" With that she pushed up on her tiptoes and kissed Joe chastely on the forehead.

"Sure, I'm okay with that. After all, we are in public, and that's probably the most I'm comfortable with. I will say, I would be comfortable with something even more passionate in private. That is, if you're comfortable with that."

"I might be comfortable with that," Ruby grinned.

I can hear you guys, and I am not comfortable with that. George was staring out the passenger window at the two of them.

Get over it, buddy. I'm back. Joe saluted the dog behind Ruby's back. George lay down in the seat to wait for Ruby's return.

J oe selected a couple of thick rib eye steaks and some garlic rub. Ruby bought salad greens, some fresh bread dough, onions, garlic, and frozen hash browns.

"I just ate a corned beef sandwich and I'm already thinking about dinner," Joe sighed. "Hanging around you is going to make me fat." He pinched his midsection, ruefully.

"I feel your pain," Ruby commiserated. I've packed on a couple of pounds myself. I want to go for a long hike tomorrow. You want to come with me, or do you have something else planned?"

"Actually, I wanted to go up to an area called Dolly Sods and take some photographs. The weather is supposed to be good tomorrow. You want to come with me up there? It's pretty rugged, and it's supposed to be very beautiful."

"I would love to. The climbing instructor told me about that place. He told me I shouldn't miss it. In fact, he offered to take me up there." Ruby watched Joe's face. She wasn't disappointed. A cloud seemed to pass over him, but he struggled to not let it show. Ruby burst out laughing. "I thanked him, but told him I would probably go up there with my boyfriend. That would be you. You are the boyfriend."

"I like that title. Boyfriend it is. Now let's get this food back to the campers, and I vote for a nap. What do you say? By the way, do you have a hammock?"

"No, I don't. Do you?"

"I do. I use it for when I want to go camping in the woods. I don't need to carry a tent. I also use it for afternoon siestas."

"That sounds amazing. I wish I had one."

"I saw an outfitter store on the way out of town. Do you want to stop and see if you want to get one?"

"Yeah. I don't know what I'm looking for, but let's go. We have to hurry so this stuff doesn't get warm, but I'm up for it."

"It's okay. I have a cooler in the truck. I also have some cold sodas and water if you want something."

"Always prepared aren't you?"

"I try. Let's get you a hammock so we can hang side by side napping the afternoon away."

After a quick stop at the outfitters they were on their way back to the campsite, Ruby with a brand new hammock that needed breaking in.

Ruby's campsite had a couple of perfectly spaced trees, so Joe showed her how to set up her hammock. In minutes they were both swaying gently, side by side under the canopy of the trees.

Suddenly, Ruby sat up and tried to get out of her hammock.

"What's wrong?" Joe asked lazily.

"I decided that I needed a mojito before my nap. I feel that sipping a mojito in my hammock just might be the perfect way to start the afternoon siesta. Can I interest you in one?"

"Absolutely. Do you need some help?"

"I don't need help making the drinks, but I might need some suggestions on how to get out of this thing without falling on my face."

"You've got it. Just commit and go for it."

Ruby pressed the fabric under her thighs and leaned forward. The hammock swung back allowing her feet to touch the ground. She stood up and bowed.

"Voila!"

"You're a natural. Are you sure you don't need help?"

"No, thanks. You just relax. I'll be out in a minute."

Ruby emerged from her camper a few minutes later with two tall, frosty mojitos. When she leaned over Joe's hammock to hand him his drink, she discovered George curled up in the swinging bed with Joe.

Joe grinned at her.

"I think he likes it. Thanks. Do you need help getting in your hammock with the drink? Let me hold it for you."

Ruby slid in and reached over for her drink. They both took a sip and looked at each other, grinning like crazy.

"I like it better when you aren't mad at me," said Joe.

"Me, too." Ruby smiled warmly at the man who had her dog curled up next to him. This does feel right, she thought. This feels very right. She sipped her drink thinking about the other night when Joe told her he loved her. She was shocked and frightened, but, if she were to be honest with herself, she liked it.

She liked it a lot.

Chapter 49

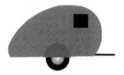

R uby woke up to the sounds of a crackling fire. She smiled and stretched. She was in love with the hammock. She rolled over and watched Joe stoking the fire. She was in love with the hammock, and she felt strongly about Joe, too.

George sat next to Joe staring up at him adoringly. What was up with that? She watched as Joe held a cheese curl up for George. The dog took it gently from his fingers, crunching it happily, his eyes closed in sheer ecstasy.

"No people food!" Ruby reminded them.

George and Joe looked over at her, the both of them looking guilty as hell.

"What do you need in order to get your food ready for dinner?" asked Joe.

"A bunch of hot coals for the bread and for the potatoes. Hang on and I'll get them started."

They worked side by side in Ruby's little kitchen. Ruby got Joe started on making dough balls for the garlic monkey bread while she prepared the hash brown and onion foil packets. Then everything was ready, Joe put the Dutch oven with the monkey bread on the coals, placing some on the top, and Ruby put the foil packets on the grill over the hot coals from the fire. Joe got the steaks out to come to room temperature and rubbed them with fresh garlic. Then they shared another mojito while they waited for the bread and potatoes to cook.

Fifteen minutes later, Joe threw the steaks on the grill and Ruby made the salad. Soon they sat down to eat their feast, George sitting at the picnic table next to Joe.

"Traitor," mumbled Ruby. George had the decency to look guilty.

As they ate their dinner, they made plans for the hike the next day. Then they sat around the campfire making small talk.

Around ten o'clock, Joe stood up.

"What's wrong?" Ruby asked.

"Just heading back to my trailer. Is seven o'clock too early for you?"

"No…that's fine. So, you're going back to your camper tonight?" Ruby asked, feeling let down.

"Yeah, honey. I think that's best, don't you?"

"I guess," she whispered.

"Okay, I'll see you tomorrow at seven. I'll pick you up."

Ruby watched as Joe walked away, heading back to his campsite. He never looked back. That bothered her.

George watched Joe's walk away, too. *Nice move. That got to her.*

I have no idea what you're talking about, Joe thought, smiling to himself.

Ruby was waiting at the picnic table for Joe with two go cups of hot coffee ready. He jumped out of the truck and presented her with a go cup of coffee. They looked at the coffees in each other's hands and laughed.

"Hang on, let me get a thermos," Ruby said. She unlocked the camper and took her thermos out of the cupboard. She drained the cups into the insulated bottle and locked the camper. Then she gratefully accepted the steaming cup from Joe and they toasted each other's thoughtfulness.

"Do you have everything you need?" asked Joe.

"I think so."

"Water? Water bowl for George? Snacks? Hammock? Jacket?"

"Check, check, check, check, check, and check," Ruby declared proudly. "I think we might need to rest in our hammocks at the top of a mountain, don't you?"

"I think that is a distinct possibility," Joe agreed.

Ruby got into Joe's truck and he handed her an eager George. The dog plopped happily between the two of them and looked out the front window of the truck anxious for the adventure ahead.

The day was warm, and the milky sunshine shrouded with wispy clouds was pleasant. Ruby wore a pair of hiking shorts and a mint green tank top that set off her auburn hair. The scoop neck was a bit revealing, showing the smattering of freckles across her chest. She didn't wear the shirt often, feeling a little self-conscious at how tightly it pulled across her chest, but she felt like today it might be a good day to wear it. After all, it was pleasantly warm. And Joe looked like he might need warmed up.

She noticed him glancing over at her as he drove. Yep, he was thawing. She pretended she was unaware. George looked back and forth between the two of them, growled, and laid down on the seat. He didn't want to be in the middle of their games.

The road up to Dolly Sods was steep and full of switchbacks. They reached the parking area for the trailhead where Joe had decided to start the hike. Ruby reached in the backseat for her backpack, fastened George's leash on, and opened the truck door, ready to hop out.

She was met with a blast of ice cold air. The wind was blowing sharply, and the temperature was a good thirty degrees colder. She looked over at Joe about to say something when she realized he was smirking at her, thoroughly enjoying the view. It was obvious she was cold.

Ignoring him, she deftly reached into her pack and pulled out her fleece. Without saying a word, she zipped it on and smiled sweetly at him.

"Ready to go?"

"Yes ma'am. The trail goes this way."

"They hiked through a thin woods that was full of knee deep ferns. It was like wading in a sea of green. George leaped and hopped, trying to see above the lush undergrowth but it was hopeless unless he stuck to the trail. Despite the fact that Ruby had removed his leash, he hung by her side. He wasn't fond of the ferns.

Joe, on the other hand, loved them. He worked magic with his camera, capturing the way the light wove through the fronds, making a million shades of green. Ruby waited patiently as he worked. She loved watching him. Sometimes it was hard to remember he was an artist because he had such a rugged man look. It was a whole different dimension to his character that she thought maybe most people didn't see. She felt it was a privilege to be part of it. Her heart swelled in her chest. This man had so many facets. He was so good and kind.

Joe took that moment to look back at her, his smile dazzling. She returned it in kind. There was a moment. Electricity in the air. They stood there smiling amid the sea of ferns, and Ruby felt like there was something really right with this.

In a second, he was by her side. He took her hand and led

her down the trail at an easy pace, George keeping up on the other side of Ruby.

The trail turned and began a steep incline. They climbed steadily for another hour, the vegetation getting thinner. Soon, it was a completely different world. The trees were stunted and twisted. Low lying bushes which were full of tiny blueberries clung tenaciously to the rocks. They were a testament to survival as they continued to produce fruit year after punishing year, exposed to the harsh elements that Dolly Sods threw at them.

Joe spent some time on the cliffs taking more pictures. He snapped a few of Ruby without her knowing. He knew he got some good ones and he was pleased. He was thinking about the day that they would have to go their separate ways, and he wasn't looking forward to it. He didn't want it to happen, but he know that she didn't owe him anything. He just wanted to have some good pictures to remember her by.

They moved on, discovering cranberry bogs, ground so spongey that if they stood too long, they began to sink. After hiking on the loose rocks earlier, the loamy earth was a welcome relief.

Another hour passed, and the sun broke through the clouds lighting up the sods with dazzling colors. The wind had died down, and the day was a little warmer. They stopped on the side of a cliff in a sheltered area where the sun warmed the rocks around them. Three perfect trees stood in a triangle, perfect for hanging two hammocks side by side. Ruby hung them while Joe set out lunch. They sat on the warm rocks and ate cured summer sausage with hard aged cheddar, hummus, and some soft pita bread. Ruby produced two candy bars and they polished them down with some tea Ruby had brewed in her water bottle as she hiked.

"Time for a siesta on the side of this amazing cliff?" Joe asked Ruby.

"Past time," she said, as she stretched out in the suspended bed and relaxed completely.

"I'll be with you in just a minute," said Joe as he stepped into the bushes.

As he came out, he grabbed his camera. He couldn't believe how beautiful Ruby was, lying in her hammock, her glorious hair spread around her. The cliff dropped off just past the trees, and the vista spread behind her made an amazing backdrop. He snapped a dozen pictures before he was satisfied. Then he quietly crept up to her. She was asleep, a slight smile playing on her lips. Her cheeks were pink from the wind and the sun. He took a couple of closeups of her sleeping, feeling a little like an interloper, but not really caring. He wanted to capture that look forever.

Satisfied, he carefully stowed his camera in the padded case in his bag and zipped it closed. He hung his pack at the head of this hammock, so it was in easy reach. George was sitting on the ground looking pointedly at the hammock.

Joe scooped him up and placed him gently in Ruby's hammock. George thumped his tail happily and snuggled up next to his Ruby. Joe crawled into his own hammock. They both moved around until they were comfortable. Within minutes, all three of them fell asleep.

Chapter 50

George's head snapped up, pulling out of a sound sleep, a growl deep and threatening emanated from his chest.

Joe, did you hear that? What is it? George growled again, louder this time, his hackles raised.

Joe stopped snoring.

Sighed.

Joe!

Joe started snoring again.

Danger was near. It was eminent, and George was scared.

Closer.

The threat was closer.

JOE!

George flew out of Ruby's hammock and crashed into the underbrush. Nothing was going to hurt his Ruby. Not ever.

Joe and Ruby slept on, cradled in their gently swaying wombs.

George charged through the undergrowth, instinct leading him. He emerged from the edge of the forest into a clearing, confronting the large black bear that spun around to meet his attacker. Furious and seeing red, George showed no fear as he charged the bear. The bruin reared onto his hind legs as George attempted to drive him back into the forest and away from his humans. The bear swiped at George, but the dog dodged. Although the bear missed making a direct hit, his claw snagged George's collar, slicing his neck and hooking the leather. The little dog dangled in the air, choking and twisting, the collar cutting off his air. The bear shook his paw, trying to free his claw from the annoying terrier. That just tightened the collar harder against the dog's neck. As the light started to fade in front of George's eyes, the collar slipped from his neck, and he plummeted to the ground. Angry, George shook himself and launched himself straight at the bear. The next thing he knew, the animal's giant paw slammed into him mid-leap, sending him flying through the air and over the edge of the nearby embankment.

George hit the slope and rolled down a hundred feet into the valley below, stopping against a rock at the base of the cliff.

He didn't move.

The wind shifted, bringing the scent of humans to the bear. He didn't want anything to do with people. His last encounter left him with a bullet lodged in his left hip. Humans meant pain, and he wasn't interested. He hurried down the path in the opposite direction, no longer concerned with the dog, only interested in putting as much distance between himself and the humans and possible.

J oe sat up in his hammock. Something was wrong. His head snapped over to Ruby. She was sleeping soundly. She was fine.

Something.

George.

Where was George?

Joe swung out of the hammock and whistled softly. He didn't want to alarm Ruby, and George was sure to come trotting out of the woods having finished his business.

No George.

He whistled again.

Ruby stretched in her hammock.

Joe whistled one more time.

"Where's George?" Ruby asked, no real concern in her voice.

"Probably just stretching his legs. I'm sure he'll be back in a minute. Did you have a nice nap?"

"It was wonderful, but I'm a little chilly. I'll warm up once we get moving again." She rubbed her arms trying to warm up.

Joe came to her and gathered her into him. He was starting to get worried, and he was getting the feeling this day was going to end badly. Ruby melted into his arms. It felt like forever since he had held her. She was afraid things weren't going to be the same again, but this felt perfect, like she belonged. He smiled down at her.

"This feels nice," he said, savoring the moment.

"Yeah, it does. Now where is that dog? I'm getting hungry. Are you?"

"A little. Let's get these hammocks down and go find George."

Ruby called for her dog as she unhooked the hammock from the tree straps and crammed it into the small stuff sack.

Then she pulled the straps off the tree, putting them in their stow bag. She kept looking around for her dog.

"George, come on buddy. Let's go," she called.

Joe whistled for the dog as he put the last of his things in his backpack. He was now getting seriously concerned.

"Joe, I don't understand why George isn't coming when we call. He never does that. Never. Where was he when you got into your hammock? I was already asleep and never saw you get into it."

"I picked him up and put him in with you. He snuggled up behind your bent knees and wagged his tail. Then I climbed into my hammock and was out like a light."

"I just don't get it." Panic was starting to show in Ruby's voice.

"Hey, don't worry. We'll find him. He probably chased a chipmunk or something."

They hoisted their packs and started moving down the trail in the direction they had come calling for George, at first in a normal voice, but when there was no response, they increased the volume.

Ruby stopped in the middle of the trail after they had gone a quarter of a mile. She turned back toward the clearing where they had stopped.

"Joe, I'm going back. George would never have just taken off. What makes us think he's on this trail?"

"I don't know, honey. We can go back and maybe head up the trail in the other direction. Maybe he went that way."

They hiked in silence, each worrying, not wanting the other to know just how concerned they were. Ruby was trying to be brave, but tears were threatening to spill.

They continued calling for George as they explored the trail that continued on from where they took their nap. Still nothing.

Clouds were moving in, sweeping up the mountain, lifting from the valley. Droplets of moisture hung in the air.

The temperature was dropping.

Ruby shivered.

"Honey, you're cold. Stop and put on your jacket before you get any colder."

Silently, Ruby pulled her puffy jacket out of her backpack and put it on. Somehow, she didn't think it was going to stop the chill she was feeling in the pit of her stomach.

Half a mile later, they turned around again. Ruby's shoulders were slumped in defeat and worry. When they reached the clearing again, Ruby dropped her backpack and started digging in it.

"What are you looking for?" asked Joe.

"I'm setting up my hammock again."

"Why?"

"I'm going to make camp for the night. I'm going to wait for him right here, right where he knows we are. I'm not leaving him. He'll come back to me."

"Ruby, honey, you don't have what you need to make camp."

"Why not?" Ruby fired back, defiantly. "You said you use your hammock when you want to camp in the woods."

"I do, but I use a tarp above me to provide me shelter, and I use a sleeping bag to keep warm. You have no way of staying warm. You're already shivering."

"I have my coat. I'll be fine."

"No, you won't be fine," Joe said sternly. "If you try to spend the night in your hammock tonight without a sleeping bag, you'll die of hyperthermia. That's not gonna happen."

Ruby's jaw tightened. She was scared and felt helpless, so she was ready to fight.

"You don't tell me what to do. I will not leave my dog. I'll stay right here until he comes back. You're welcome to stay with me or not. It doesn't matter to me one way or another."

Her feet were planted shoulder width apart, her fists on her hips, and a scowl on her face. If Joe wasn't so worried, he would've laughed at the beautiful, tough woman before him.

Once again, he drew her into his arms. At first, she resisted, but then she yielded and allowed him to comfort her, stroking her hair and murmuring encouraging words as his own mind conjured up all the horrible things that could have happened to the scrappy little dog.

After a few minutes, Joe pulled away from Ruby. He pushed the hair away from her face and tilted her chin.

"I'm going to do everything I can to find him. I promise. Let's think and do this logically. We made a mess of this area by walking back and forth a bunch of times, but let's check the perimeter and look for his tracks. Maybe we can figure out where he went and what happened to him."

With a task to complete, Ruby tried to put her worry aside and got to work. They followed around the clearing systematically, looking closely at the ground trying to find any trace of dog footprints that might be there.

About fifteen minutes later, Ruby called out excitedly,

"Joe, come here. Aren't these dog footprints?"

Joe hurried over and looked where she was pointing. There were some prints that looked like small dog, perhaps one that was in a hurry. The front of the print and the claws were dug in deeper as if the dog had launched forward in a leap or was running.

"I think so. I never learned the art of tracking, but I think we can conclude these are George's. Let's see if we can follow them. It looks like he went straight into the underbrush here."

They pushed their way through the brush, occasionally finding a paw print. In a few minutes they came out into another clearing well off the trail.

"Joe, look!" Ruby ran forward into the center of the clearing and scooped up a small object. "His collar!" she said triumphantly.

As Joe hurried over, she turned the collar over in her open hand. Her palm was covered in blood.

"Joe," Ruby whispered.

The color drained from her face.

"Oh my God, Joe." Ruby swayed on her feet, and Joe deftly caught her. She clung to him, the collar clutched tightly in her hand, and sobbed.

Joe tried to comfort her, but at the same time he glanced around them. There still might be some danger about, and he didn't want to be caught by surprise.

He didn't see any sign of anything out of the ordinary as he scanned the woods around him.

Ruby leaned into him, trembling with fear.

"What happened to him? Where is he? Why is there all this blood?" she asked, looking for him to make sense of everything.

Joe was at a loss. He had no idea how to answer, or what to say.

"We have to find him. We have to help him." Ruby pushed herself away from Joe. "I'm going to find my dog." As she moved to step away from Joe, he looked at the ground where Ruby had found the collar. What he saw made his blood run cold.

He squatted down and looked carefully at the dirt. He was no tracker, but it was obvious some type of tussle had happened here. There were blood spots in the dirt and the ground was torn up. Joe slowly walked around the circle where the dirt was disturbed and finally found what he was looking for. A set of tracks leading away. Only one set of tracks. One set of very large tracks.

Bear.

And no tracks from a dog. It was as if the dog had disappeared from that spot. Joe didn't want to think about what the bear did to the little dog.

"Joe, what is it?" Ruby had the bloody collar clutched to her chest.

Joe just stared at her. How was he going to tell her? He wasn't sure. There was no concrete evidence that the bear had eaten the dog. There would have been more blood. And scraps. And fur.

But there was a very good chance that the bear had carried the dog away with him. What other explanation could there be? There were no dog footprints leading away. None.

Joe walked the perimeter again, postponing answering Ruby.

"Joe, talk to me," she begged.

His heart broke. There were no more dog tracks.

He took her in his arms and explained what he thought as gently as he could.

Ruby stumbled her way back to the truck, hiking the miles in silence, tears running down her cheeks. At first, she refused to believe what Joe told her. Then she got angry. She yelled. She accused him of hating George. She called and called for her dog until her voice was hoarse. Called for a dog who never came.

"I've lost him. I lost him once. I can't lose him again. I can't."

Finally, exhausted, she turned numbly and started walking down the trail toward the truck, clutching George's collar, refusing to let go.

Chapter 51

When they got back to Ruby's trailer, Joe helped her into her Ohio University t-shirt and tucked her into bed. She lay there, staring at George's water bowl sitting lonely in the corner of the trailer by the kitchen cabinet.

She moaned.

Joe picked up the bowl and took it outside. He emptied it and left it on the picnic table. Then he stepped back into the camper, removed his shoes, and crawled into bed behind Ruby. He pulled her tight up against him wrapping both arms around her, encircling her with warmth. He knew he couldn't fix it. All he could do was love her and hope that she could heal.

He knew she wasn't sleeping. He could hear her crying quietly, but he kept silent and held her.

Eventually, they slept.

S omething.
Joe woke.

He was disoriented.

He took a minute and realized Ruby was still wrapped in his arms.

Something woke him, but it wasn't Ruby. She was still sleeping.

Joe, I've lost your scent. I can't find my way back.

Joe shook his head. He was dreaming. He blinked his eyes and pulled Ruby even closer, tucking her head neatly under his chin. He, too, was mourning the loss of the little dog.

Joe, I'm lost. I followed your scent for a while, but it's gone, and I'm cold.

Joe carefully crawled out of bed, tucking the blankets securely around Ruby's shoulders, swaddling her in his remaining warmth.

He pulled on his shoes and shrugged on his coat. He picked up his pack and the bag of cheese curls off the counter.

I'm coming, buddy. I'll find you. Just hang on.

J oe closed the camper door as quietly as he could, worried he would wake her. He peeked in the camper window where the curtain was open a sliver, just to check on her. She hadn't moved.

Getting in his truck he started the engine and drove away, pulling the door closed after he was away from the camper. He hoped he hadn't awakened her.

George, where are you? I need to find you.

Nothing.

Joe scowled into the night as he headed out of the campground and turned toward the road that led to the Dolly Sods access road. What if he imagined it? He could be on a wild goose chase. Dolly Sods was miles away. How could he connect with the dog all the way over there, and why hadn't it happened sooner? What if it was just a dream?

It bothered him to leave Ruby alone. He didn't leave a note. What was going to happen when she woke up and he wasn't there? Especially after losing George. Maybe he should turn back.

I'm really cold, Joe. And my side and neck hurt a lot. I need help.

I'm coming, buddy. I just don't know where.

He drove into the night, slowing at each service road, trying to find the one they had driven earlier. It was easy to find during the day, but night time was another issue. Wait, there it was.

Joe turned on the road and headed up the mountain.

The headlights cast shadows, making tree branches look like animals darting in front of the truck. The lane was narrow. It seemed narrower in the dark. Dodging the potholes was easier in the daylight, too. He drove up and up, trying to remember how long it took them to get to the trailhead. Time moved faster with Ruby. He missed her next to him.

He found a pull-off and moved the truck into it, but when he got out, it didn't seem familiar. He hiked over to the trail opening but the sign was all wrong. This wasn't the one they took earlier.

He got back in the truck and looked at his map. The next turn off was the one he wanted. He started up the road again, praying he would be able to find George and that the dog would be okay. He wanted so badly to bring that damn terrier back into Ruby's arms.

He snorted to himself. Here he was, out in the middle of

the night, looking for the dog that represented the dead husband of the woman he loved. If that wasn't messed up.

It may be messed up, but you like me, and you know it, and Ruby loves me, so you're stuck. Now hurry the hell up. I'm really cold...

Joe pushed the truck faster and was rewarded by hitting a large pot hole and hitting his head on the roof of the truck.

"Damn it," he yelled in frustration.

The turn off was just ahead. He swung in and threw the truck in park. As he stepped out, he was shocked at just how cold it was. The few hundred feet he had gained since the last turn off had really changed the air temperature. And Ruby wanted to try to stay in the hammock waiting for George. She would have been hyperthermic by now, he thought.

"George," Joe yelled, following with a whistle. "Where are you, buddy?"

Joe peered into the darkness, then turned and reached back into his truck for his powerful flashlight.

He swung it around, peering into the underbrush before he turned toward the trail.

"George. Here boy. Come on buddy!" Joe worked his way up the trail.

"George!"

Stop yelling, I'm right here.

"George?" Joe said softly.

He listened.

He heard a soft whine.

He swept the flashlight back and forth in front of him.

There.

The reflection of eyes.

"George?"

A yip.

Joe moved quickly in the direction of the eyes. There, shivering under a low bush was George.

The dog blinked at the strong light shining in his face.

Dude!

"Sorry, buddy." Joe crouched down and looked over the dog. He was caked in blood.

"George, you look pretty rough. Took on the wrong guy, huh?"

Joe stripped his coat off and covered the dog.

George thumped his tail, gratefully.

Hey, Joe. Have you ever been close up to a bear?

"No, buddy, I can't say I have."

Well, don't do it. They stink.

Joe gathered the dog in his arms and lifted him gently.

George cried out in a painful yelp.

"What's wrong, buddy? What hurts? Your neck is torn open. That's got to hurt some."

My side hurts worse. George's tongue rapidly licked Joe's hand as if trying to heal his hurt by licking Joe.

"I'll try to be careful."

Joe carried George to his truck.

"I have to open the door. I don't want to hurt you. I'll try to be careful." He hugged the dog against him with one arm and opened the passenger door. George stiffened but stayed quiet.

Joe hurried to the other side and got in the driver's side. He checked his phone to see if he had any service.

Nothing.

"Okay, buddy. We're driving into Elkins. Maybe we can find some vet services somewhere." In the middle of the night. In the mountains. Fat chance.

He drove down the mountain, doing the best he could to avoid the potholes. When he hit them, sometimes George would whimper, but most of the time, he remained stoic.

When they hit the main road, Joe turned toward town. He thought about stopping for Ruby.

Don't.

"Okay, buddy. Just hang in there."

235

As he drove, he kept checking his cell phone. As he came up out of a valley and reached the top of the mountains on the main road, suddenly he had service. The phone pinged with incoming emails. Quickly, Joe pulled to the side of the road and checked to see if he could find any emergency vet services. The service was painfully slow, but eventually he found what he was looking for. He dialed the number. An on-call vet tech answered the phone. Joe quickly explained that his dog was attacked by a bear and was suffering exposure, a torn neck, and possible internal injuries. He was told to bring the dog in and was given the address.

"I'm getting you help. Just hang on, George."

This time, there was no response.

Joe pushed the truck faster, flying down the mountains and into town. Not knowing where the clinic was, he had to stop again and put the address in his GPS. He was cursing out loud and sweating, frustrated that it was taking so much time.

Finally, he pulled into a well-lit parking lot. As he reached the door, a staff member opened it for him and led him into an examining room. Then, just like in a people hospital, a tech led him out of the room and closed the door. An office worker took him to her desk and had him start filling out forms.

When they asked for payment in advance, Joe panicked, afraid that he had left his wallet at Ruby's, but after searching the pocket of the bloody coat that had been wrapped around George, he found it.

Joe handed over his credit card, then sat to wait for the verdict. He debated calling Ruby, but then remembered that there wasn't any cell service in the campground. He prayed she was still sleeping. He hated the idea of her waking up and thinking he had left her.

Chapter 52

"E xcuse me, sir?"

Joe startled awake.

"You can come back and see your dog, now." The young vet tech smiled at Joe. "He's going to be fine."

Joe followed the tech while trying to clear the cobwebs from his head.

"Hey buddy," Joe greeted George.

The dog thumped his tail and grinned at Joe, a big, sloppy, doggy grin.

"Are you stoned?" Joe asked the dog.

There that tail went again. Thump. Thump. Thump.

There was still a little blood left on his neck, but he was cleaned up and looking a lot better than when Joe had walked out of this room. There was an area on his neck that was shaved and stitched, and there was a spot on his front leg that was also shaved.

The vet walked over and shook Joe's hand.

"George here is going to be okay, but you need to keep him quiet for a few days. He has some cracked ribs, and he's pretty banged up. I stitched up the tear in his neck and gave him some antibiotics. Bear claws are nasty things, full of bacteria. Did you see the bear attack him?"

"No,"

"Then how did you know it was a bear?" the vet asked absently, as he wrote on a form.

"He told me," Joe said, not thinking as he scratched George's ears.

The vet stopped writing and looked at Joe, shrugged and went back to what he was doing.

"So, he's going to need to stay on these antibiotics. Don't miss a dose. They may upset his stomach a bit, but keep him on the meds. Here are some pain killers. He's on some of those now, as you so astutely observed earlier. They will help ease the pain. I have all the instructions written down. You need to keep him quiet and let him heal. Give him a few sips of water when you get back to wherever you are staying. If he feels like eating, just give him a little at a time. We really don't want him throwing up. Any questions?"

"When do the stitches come out?"

"Ten days. You can do it if you have the stomach for it. If not, any vet will be happy to help you. You're traveling, right?"

"Yes, we are. I think I can manage to take them out. Is there anything else?"

"Yeah, don't forget to pick up your credit card. I'm sure Mabel is done abusing it by now. Sorry about the cost of emergency pet care, but it's what keeps the doors open for situations just like these," the vet said cheerfully. "Call me if you have any questions and have a good night." The vet shook his hand again and disappeared out the door.

Joe put the medications and instructions in his pants pocket and gently wrapped the dog in his coat.

On the way out, he picked up his card from Mabel. She grinned at him and thanked him, then helped him open the door to the clinic and his truck. She was a nice lady, despite what she just did to his credit card.

George snuggled down into the coat with a sigh and promptly fell asleep. Dawn was on it's way, and on the road out of town Joe passed a bakery that had just opened its doors. He pulled in and left a sleeping George on the seat. As he opened the door of the bakery, the heady scent of fresh cinnamon rolls hit him hard. He bought a dozen and two cups of strong, hot coffee.

Back in the truck, George didn't even wiggle his nose at the smell of the cinnamon rolls. Joe, however, devoured one in two bites. He sipped his hot coffee and wrapped his stocking cap around the one he bought for Ruby, hoping to keep it warm on the ride back to her camper. He couldn't wait to see the look on her face when she saw he had brought her coffee, cinnamon rolls, and her little dog, too.

J oe pulled in behind Ruby's Jeep. George raised his head.

"We're home, buddy. Ready to surprise Ruby?"

The dog thumped his tail feebly. He was tired and was having difficulty matching Joe's enthusiasm.

Joe got out of the truck and moved to the passenger side. He opened the door and carefully gathered George in his arms. This time, the dog didn't make a sound and remained relaxed.

"Good pills, huh?" asked Joe.

Damn good.

Joe peeked in the trailer window, looking again through the slit where the curtains didn't quite close. He needed to remember to tell Ruby about that. In the dim light, he could see Ruby's form on the bed. She was curled up, her back to the door. It seemed she hadn't heard his truck.

Holding George against his chest, he used the key he snagged from the table last night and let himself in. Ruby didn't move.

George did. He wagged his tail, perking up.

Joe moved to the bed and carefully lay the dog, still wrapped in the coat, down on the bed facing Ruby.

Ruby didn't move.

"Ruby?" Joe said softly, worried.

She's still breathing, dude. Relax.

Damn you dog. Do you know freaking everything?

Pretty much. George wiggled out of the coat and pulled himself up to Ruby's chin. His little pink tongue flicked out and licked her gently.

Ruby protested.

George licked some more.

"SERIOUSLY JOE, DO YOU HAVE NO DECENCY?" Ruby cried out in a sharp voice.

"I would certainly hope you could tell the difference between my tongue and a dog's," Joe replied laughing.

Ruby's eyes flew open, and George threw himself into a licking frenzy, covering her face with spit.

"Um, I think the meds are making him drool more than usual," Joe laughed.

"Oh my God, George! Where? How? I thought I'd lost you! I thought you were dead!" She moved her arms around the little dog to pull him closer, but Joe stopped her.

"Hang on. He's hurt. We spent the night at the emergency veterinarian. George has some healing to do. Pet him gently, and I'll be right back."

Joe left the two of them to their reunion while he went back out to the truck to retrieve Ruby's coffee and the remaining cinnamon rolls.

When he came back, he found Ruby inspecting every inch

of George's body. George's eyes were closed loving every bit of attention.

"Coffee that is not quite piping hot, and some fresh cinnamon rolls?"

"Joe, I love you."

Joe turned from the counter and stared at Ruby.

There were tears in her eyes, and George was looking at Joe, wagging his tail as hard as he could.

"Are you going to say anything? Are you mad? Do you still love me, because Joe, I love you so much. I don't know what all you did last night, how you found George, but even without that, I realized that I love you, and I don't want to be without you. I hope I'm not too late."

Joe crossed the trailer and crouched in front of the bed, one arm around Ruby and the other around George.

"Ruby, I love both of you. I can't imagine my life without you or your damn dog. It's not too late. It's just starting."

George barked.

Joe pulled Ruby to him and kissed her thoroughly,

George growled, then smiled his happy dog smile.

"By the way, your dog now does drugs," Joe told Ruby as he nuzzled her neck.

"Okay, I really think I need to catch up. But those cinnamon rolls smell amazing, and we never ate anything last night. Let's start with those then move on to some eggs and bacon. Then you can tell me about the adventures my two favorite guys had last night. And when you're done, you can tell me just how much I owe you, 'cause I think last night may have cost you a fortune."

"No kidding, but I don't want cash for it. I can think of a million other ways for you to pay me back!"

Joe kissed the top of her head and moved back into the kitchen, pulling out the cinnamon rolls and handing Ruby her coffee.

She turned to see if George was still comfortable, but he had already fallen asleep. Slipping on a pair of shorts and her flip flops, she carried her coffee and two plates out to the picnic table. Joe followed her with the rolls. They watched morning light up the mountains while they ate, and Joe filled her in on just what had happened while she slept.

Chapter 53

The late afternoon found Ruby in Joe's arms, George tucked between their legs, all tangled together in the bed in Ruby's camper. George barked softly. He needed to go out, but he hurt too badly to think about jumping off the bed.

Joe opened one eye and glared at the dog.

Remind me why I saved you.

The dog just smiled sweetly at Joe and waited patiently, knowing Joe would take care of him. He was not mistaken.

When Joe came back in the camper after watching George outside, Ruby was already up and had started making dinner The camper was filled with the heady aroma of sautéing butter and salty country ham.

"Mmmm. I could get used to this," Joe murmured into Ruby's hair as he hugged her from behind.

"Me, too. Did you have a nice nap?" Ruby asked as she turned to kiss Joe, wrapping her arms around his neck. The ham crackled in the skillet behind her.

"I did. Did you?"

Ruby nodded, pressing her lips against his again.

Let's not get carried away. We'll ruin dinner, and I'm hungry, besides, George is watching."

They both looked over to the bed where George was licking the shaved spot on his forearm.

He looked up and growled at them with a smile on his face.

"George, you're a goof!" Ruby laughed and turned back to the stove. "I hope you don't mind instant mashed potatoes, I'm running low on supplies. You like redeye gravy?"

"Never had it, but I am willing to try, and instant mashed potatoes are just fine."

They worked together to make dinner, then once again left George to sleep a second time that day while they went outside to eat.

🌲

"So, what's next?" Ruby asked, while she chewed thoughtfully on a salty piece of country ham.

"I was going to ask you the same thing."

"Well, I should head home and check in with my editor. I'd also like Rich, my vet friend to look George over. "

"You don't trust me to take his stitches out when the time comes, do you?"

"No, that's not it. I just would feel better if Rich would give him the once over. I appreciate all you did, what you did, but I wasn't there. I can't explain it. I'm sorry, I'm not making sense."

"No, you are. You just want to be sure you've done your best for who you love. You won't have closure until you do, so we're going to see this Rich character."

"What about you? Don't you have any commitments?"

"I do, but nothing pressing. In a week or so, I should go home and meet up with my sister. It'll be her birthday, so I should probably be nice."

"You have a sister?"

"Yeah. Why are you surprised?"

"Because I really don't know anything about you."

"You know that you love me and that's all that matters. Oh yeah, and my sister is a bitch."

"Wow, that's not a very nice thing to say about your sister."

"No, she's quite proud of it. She hates men, too."

"All men, or just specific ones?"

"Let's just say she will use them to fulfill a basic need, then discard them like a used tissue."

"She should meet Adam," Ruby murmured.

"What's that?" asked Joe as he scraped his plate clean.

"Just a guy I know. He's super nice. A great guy, but not interested in a commitment. Likes friends with benefits, but no strings. Really a nice guy though."

"Who are you trying to convince?"

Ruby laughed. "No one. He really is nice. He used me, took me to dinner once so he could show his sister that he isn't gay. She wants him to have a girlfriend. I accepted that part for an evening. I got a nice dinner and an annoying dog out of the deal."

"Ah, the forest ranger."

"Exactly. Maybe we'll see him when we go to see Rich. They're good friends."

"Works for me. I'll make it abundantly clear to both of them that you are no longer available."

Ruby leaned over the table and put her hand on the back of Joe's head, pulling him to her. She kissed him and stood up.

"I'm going to check on George and make a mojito. Need anything? A mojito of your own perhaps?"

"If you're offering, I'm drinking."

"I'm offering. Stick with me and you'll have all the mojitos you could possible want."

Sign up for Lark's newsletter

Would you like to know when Lark releases her next book? Do you want a sneak peek at sample chapters? If so, sign up for Lark Griffing's newsletter.

Subscribe now

Or use this URL to subscribe

http://eepurl.com/dH1mzz

Also by Lark Griffing

Gone To the Dogs Camper Romance Series

Teardrops and Flip Flops

Young adult novels:

The Last Time I Checked I Was Still Here

The Starfish Talisman

Short Story Collections

Dog on the Doorstep

Twelve Tales A'Telling

About the Author

Lark Griffing likes to bring her sense of adventure to her writing. Her first two novels are young adult; *The Last Time I Checked, I Was Still Here,* a coming of age story and *The Starfish Talisman,* an old-fashioned ghost story.

Dog on the Doorstep is Lark's collection of short stories and flash fiction for the holiday season about hope and the love of pets. She is also a contributor to the short story anthology *Twelve Tales A-Telling: a Modern Twist on a Holiday Classic.*

Teardrops and Rest Stops is the second novel is the first novel of her new romantic comedy series, A Gone To the Dogs Camper Romance. *Teardrops and Rest Stops* is the second in the series.

Lark collects hobbies like some people collect friends. When not writing and teaching, she is hiking, kayaking, SCUBA diving, camping, and enjoying life to the fullest with her family. She is married to a wonderful man and has two sons. She also shares her home with a precocious golden doodle, Maggie and a tabby cat, Dickens.

facebook.com/larkgriffing

twitter.com/Lark_Griffing

instagram.com/LarkGriffing